COCKY BROTHER

ANNABELLE ANDERS

Cocky Earl — "JULES" EARL OF WESTERLEY
Marries Charley Jackson

Cocky Baron — "CHASE" BARON CHASWICK
Marries Bethany Fitzwilliam

Cocky Mister — "STONE" MR. STONE SPENCER
Marries Tabetha Fitzwilliam

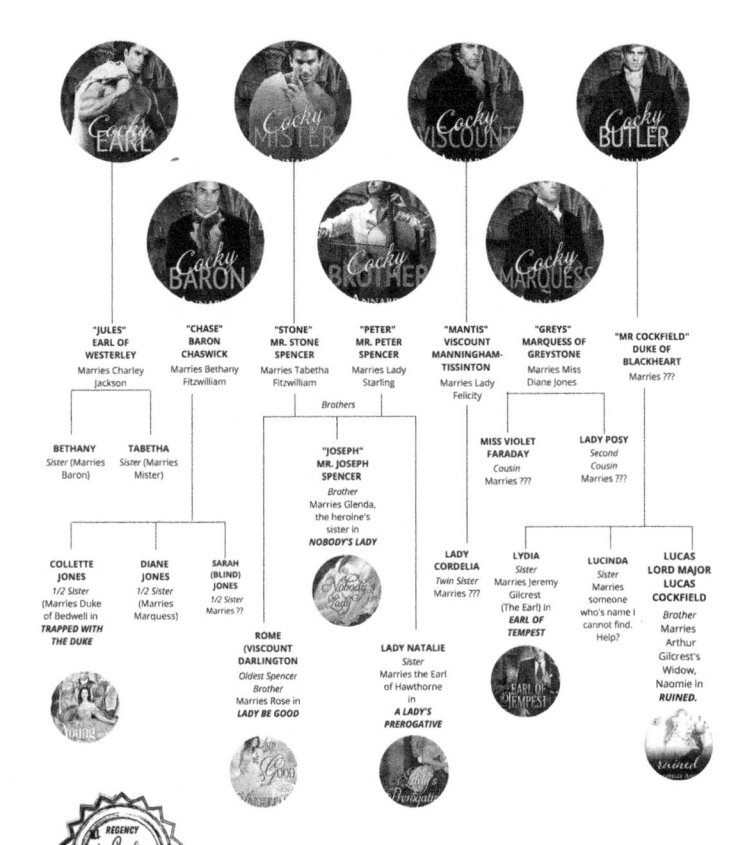

Cocky Brother — "PETER" MR. PETER SPENCER
Marries Lady Starling

Cocky Viscount — "MANTIS" VISCOUNT MANNINGHAM-TISSINTON
Marries Lady Felicity

Cocky Marquess — "GREYS" MARQUESS OF GREYSTONE
Marries Miss Diane Jones

Cocky Butler — "MR COCKFIELD" DUKE OF BLACKHEART
Marries ???

Brothers (Stone & Peter Spencer)

"JOSEPH" MR. JOSEPH SPENCER
Brother
Marries Glenda, the heroine's sister in *NOBODY'S LADY*

BETHANY — Sister (Marries Baron)
TABETHA — Sister (Marries Mister)

COLLETTE JONES — 1/2 Sister (Marries Duke of Bedwel in *TRAPPED WITH THE DUKE*)
DIANE JONES — 1/2 Sister (Marries Marquess)
SARAH (BLIND) JONES — 1/2 Sister Marries ??

ROME (VISCOUNT DARLINGTON)
Oldest Spencer Brother
Marries Rose in *LADY BE GOOD*

LADY NATALIE
Sister
Marries the Earl of Hawthorne in *A LADY'S PREROGATIVE*

MISS VIOLET FARADAY — Cousin Marries ???
LADY POSY — Second Cousin Marries ???

LADY CORDELIA
Twin Sister
Marries ???

LYDIA
Sister
Marries Jeremy Gilcrest (The Earl) in *EARL OF TEMPEST*

LUCINDA
Sister
Marries someone who's name I cannot find. Help?

LUCAS LORD MAJOR LUCAS COCKFIELD
Brother
Marries Arthur Gilcrest's Widow, Naomie in *RUINED.*

REGENCY Cocky Gents

CONTENTS

Cocky Brother/ formerly Mayfair Maiden   vii

1. The Widowed Countess   1
2. Friction   13
3. Driving   24
4. Torn   37
5. Meandering   46
6. It Moves Me   55
7. Remember Me   64
8. Shifting Hearts   69
9. Brighton   77
10. Waiting   89
11. You Didn't Come   93
    Epilogue   103

Regency Cocky Gents   111
About the Author   113
Get a free book   115

Copyright © 2021 by Annabelle Anders

All rights reserved. Except as permitted under the U.S. Copyright Act of 1976, no part of this book may be reproduced, distributed, transmitted in any form or by any means, or stored in a database or retrieval system, without written permission from the author.

Annabelle Anders

www.annabelleanders.com

Editing by Tracy Mooring Liebchen

The characters and events in this book are fictitious. Names, characters, places, and plots are a product of the author's imagination. Any similarity to real persons, living or dead, is coincidental and not intended by the author.

❦ Created with Vellum

COCKY BROTHER/ FORMERLY MAYFAIR MAIDEN

Mr. Peter Spencer isn't interested in anything but his music, until, that is, a most unlikely lady touches his soul. Lady Starling has lost hope and faith in everything around her. Can Mr. Spencer's love bring back the magic of Christmas or will the cynical widow fail to see the gift that's right before her eyes?

(Peter Spencer appears in two of my other series: Regency Cocky Gents and Lord Love a Lady)

THE WIDOWED COUNTESS

*P*eter Spencer, third son of the Earl of Ravensdale, leaned forward in his chair and slid his left hand downward, his fingers ghosting over the strings as his thumb caressed the smooth wood that made up the neck of his cello.

Without question, he felt more comfortable with the curved instrument resting snugly between his legs than he felt doing almost anything else. He didn't require an audience. He didn't require praise. And yet…

Blood thrummed through his veins. In less than one week, he would be studying under the finest cellist in all of England. Skimming his gaze around the perimeter of the gilded ballroom, he smiled to himself. He would not miss London society over the next six months. He'd never truly fit in with the other gents, playing cards, wagering, and pursuing other gentlemanly and not-so-gentlemanly entertainments. He'd wanted something else—more.

Only a few lingering guests remained milling about the parquet floor, most having moved into the adjacent hall where supper was being served. There would be dancing after, but he'd fulfilled his obligation as a guest musician for the evening, leaving him free to bow out if he wished. If left to him, he would decline these invitations altogether. His mother, however, had a most annoying habit of accepting such engagements on his behalf.

He plucked a soft arpeggio, contemplating the farewell party his brother threatened to throw the night before he was to depart. Stone had mentioned scotch, cards, and a brothel—not necessarily in that order.

For God's sake, it wasn't as though Peter was getting married. He was simply moving to Brighton.

Golden-red flashed across the room. Not fire, but it might as well be.

The widowed Countess Starling. She stood nearby, partially hidden by a large column, staring out the terrace windows, hugging her arms in front of herself.

This lady was living proof that beauty and wealth didn't necessarily bring happiness. Earlier, from his vantage point on the dais, he'd observed a cluster of popular ladies blatantly give her the cut direct. She'd handled it well, lifting her chin and moving along, not missing a step.

But he'd seen it. The hurt, the almost imperceptible shudder of pain. And now, rather than follow the crowd into the supper-room, she held back.

As though sensing his perusal, she turned and met his gaze. Forest-green eyes, alabaster skin, and an hourglass shape to rival all figures.

He rose. "My Lady." He balanced Rosa on her endpin as he acknowledged the dazzling widow. Since the first time he'd met Lady Starling last summer at one of his mother's house parties, she had intrigued him. To be perfectly honest, she'd also plagued a few of his dreams.

Not only because of her beauty. Plentiful nubile young beauties paraded themselves in society and hardly any of them ever captured his attention beyond a fleeting appreciation.

No, Lady Starling intrigued him because of her failed potential. She reminded him of a perfectly constructed violin that no one had ever bothered to tune.

Unfortunately, she also intimidated the hell out of him.

"Do you ever dance?" Her cool voice echoed in the empty hall.

Peter narrowed his eyes and pushed back a wayward lock of hair. She didn't appear to be hinting that she was seeking him out as an escort.

"On occasion, but I prefer this side of the dance floor." He indicated the small box where the orchestra played.

Her closed posture tugged at him, evoking a myriad of conflicting emotions.

Pity. Desire. And something else. Something he couldn't quite put his finger on.

Peter ignored the urge to settle his gaze on her full bosoms or her round, inviting hips and dipped his chin to stare down at his instrument, which was a less-volatile curvaceous lady—one who would never betray him, a lady who would give her best so long as he took care of her properly.

"I hate dancing." Her voice was clipped, almost as though she was speaking to herself. "At least you have an excuse to avoid it."

He glanced up in time to see her drag a disparaging gaze

over his cello and was oddly offended on behalf of his instrument.

"I thought you were staying with your husband's family in Brighton this spring." Although her absence hadn't protected her from being involved in the latest scandal. The scandal, in fact, that led to Baron Chaswick's hasty society wedding.

"My in-laws try my patience. They were my husband's family, never mine. Nothing for me there." The droll tone of her voice hitched as she glanced toward the windows. "Perhaps nothing for me here, either."

Peter frowned, not so much at her circumstances but at his response to the pain revealed when her façade slipped.

No doubt, Lord Starling's sisters had been less than welcoming. The Earl of Starling had been thirty years his wife's senior. His family would not have accepted his widow warmly, as was usually the case when a wealthy and titled gentleman married a much younger, beautiful woman.

From what he'd heard of her sexual prowess, however, he could assume she'd kept the old man happy in his last days. His cohort, Chaswick, had attested to that after having embarked on an affair with her at a house party earlier that year.

"I've finished playing for the night," he surprised himself by saying. "Will you join me at a table in the supper-room?" He wasn't hungry. He'd intended to pack Rosa up and send for his carriage.

She shrugged, forcing a half-smile. One of those flame-colored curls fell forward, drawing Peter's attention to her expansive décolletage. "Yes. Perhaps. No."

Her ambiguous response reminded him why he'd never approached her before. It wasn't polite to sit when a lady remained standing in his presence, but the usual rules didn't apply here, did they?

He lowered himself, thinking to experiment with a particular run that had been playing through his mind. He pressed his fingers onto the strings, sliding them down, a motion that felt as familiar to him as walking.

And then Lady Starling sighed.

A melodic sigh that slid from a high 'D' to a low 'D', spanning a perfect octave. It sent a warmth down his spine and had him staring at her again, noticing the curve of her neck, feminine and fragile. And the delicate slope of her shoulders.

"A stroll through the gardens then?" Likely, she'd refuse him again.

He rubbed a hand beneath his cravat and then rolled his shoulders. Damned hot in here. Halfway through the Season, one couldn't escape the heat in even the most spectacular of Mayfair ballrooms. Especially after it had accommodated a few hundred sweating, dancing humans for several hours. Add to that the flames from all the candles...

He'd need to pack Rosa up first.

Lady Starling sent him a suspicious sideways glance. "Wouldn't you prefer to ask one of the debutantes? I'm not fooled by your musical obsession, Mister Spencer. You're one of Ravensdale's sons and sought after as much as any titled gentleman."

Peter could only laugh at that. He was the third son of an earl—granted, an incredibly wealthy earl, ensuring that he would never lack funds. But his estate, Millcot Lodge in Essex, was a modest one, and he would never hold a title.

Which was perfectly fine with him, as he was rather fond of his father and two older brothers—even if Stone had the most annoying habit of bruising his arm with the occasional brotherly punch.

"I'm not interested in strolling with a Mayfair maiden. I'm interested in strolling with *you*." Because she had no marriage-minded mama who'd be watching his every move with her daughter. It wouldn't be significant for him to be spotted alone with a widow.

But more than that. He was *interested* in her. He had been for some time now.

"Very well." It wasn't a resoundingly enthusiastic response, but he doubted the lady was ever resoundingly enthusiastic for much of anything.

"Allow me a moment to put Rosa away." Carefully setting his cello to the side, he opened the large leather case that had been custom-built to protect her for transport.

"You named it?" The question, like everything else she had said to this point, came out in mocking tones. He knew it was a part of her armor, so it didn't bother him.

"She," Peter corrected her. "She's more than a possession. She's my life. The least she deserves is a name, don't you think?"

Lady Starling's throat moved, as though his answer was difficult to swallow. "But it, pardon me, *she*, is replaceable. She's an inanimate object—wood, metal, glue."

Peter snapped the metal closures into place and stroked a hand along the leather. "But for now, she owns my heart." It was the only way he could explain how he felt about the instrument. He'd owned several others before Rosa and cared equally for each and every one of them. But for today, Rosa was the one that brought his music to life.

He moved around to the opening of the dais, vaguely

aware that Lady Starling drifted in the same direction to meet him.

"Shall I send for your wrap?" The evening was warm, but her gown might leave her catching a chill. By no means current on ladies' fashion, Peter would nonetheless wager a year's allowance that the plunging bodice of her garment challenged societal boundaries. The brilliant forest-green silk, almost identical to the color of her eyes, cinched in at her waist. The off-the-shoulder puffed sleeves draped lazily into the crooks of her elbows, where long satin gloves ended.

"I'm fine." Her answer belied her expression. She was far from fine.

Peter winged an arm. "Shall we, then?"

~

MIRANDA HATED the relief that came with tucking her hand on Peter Spencer's arm.

When had she become this pathetic creature? A person who found herself envying an inanimate object? Because seeing this gentleman lovingly secure the instrument in its velvet-lined case had all but taunted her current state of aloneness.

Pathetic indeed.

She had become *that woman*.

Beholden to no one, she did not conform to society's dictates. She acknowledged her needs and pursued avenues for fulfillment. She would not apologize for who she was.

And, because of her gender, she would forever pay the price.

Before she'd felt him watching her, she'd already been

caught in the emptiness of her need. When she'd caught him watching her, the vacuum had widened, expanded.

She wasn't so oblivious that she would fool herself into thinking he was seriously interested in her. He'd pitied her—as had nearly every other guest who'd lowered themselves to speak with her tonight. Likely, she'd be criticized for sullying this charming young man with her company.

But he wanted her. Of that, she was fairly certain.

He was younger than her thirty years, perhaps closer to five and twenty. And he had an odd innocence about him.

"Are you as angelic as people say?" she asked.

He glanced sideways at her with raised brows and for a moment, she was lost in the blue of his eyes. Not grayish-blue or greenish-blue. If a perfect blue existed, it would be the color of Peter Spencer's eyes.

"Depends on who you ask," he answered. "My mother would be inclined to say yes but any of my siblings would disagree."

She couldn't imagine having family like that.

"Do you have brothers and sisters?" he asked.

"No." She'd been raised by her widowed father. And Mrs. Lemur, her governess. "I was an only child. My mother died shortly after I was born." Their steps echoed loudly on the shining floor.

"My sympathies that you didn't know your mother but also my congratulations that you didn't have siblings to torment you." He opened the French door and gestured for her to precede him into the shadowed garden.

"I always wanted a brother or sister." Odd thing for her to tell him. But it was sweet that he'd pretend interest in her, in any of the meaningless details of her life.

His sweetness made her feel jaded—jaded at the age of thirty. And guilty that she would defile him with her need.

Before marrying Lord Starling, she'd thought she'd enjoy being a widow—being answerable to no one. And yet she'd come to depend on his company—on his affection. Her husband's death had left her feeling empty—lonely. Perhaps it was this loneliness that unhinged her tonight. One too many snubs had cracked her armor.

A breeze stirred the leaves overhead, and the murmuring voices of the guests all but disappeared when the door closed behind them.

She half-expected him to slide one hand around her waist—and then lower—she'd invited him outside alone, after all. Instead, he tucked her hand into his arm again, leading her onto a wide garden path.

He'd told her he wasn't interested in walking with a Mayfair maiden. He'd said he was interested in walking with her. Heat spread to her core as she imagined how his interest might play out. They'd walk a little farther... Would he feign romance? Kiss her first? It was easier sometimes when they did not.

Torches burned at various intervals, shedding light on the flagstone walkway. They had been spaced far enough apart, however, that a couple could easily stop in the shadows.

He would kiss her. It would not be clumsy. He embodied a gracefulness most men lacked. But would that kiss be youthful and innocent? Or did he hide a secret wickedness?

"I wouldn't trade my sister and brothers for the world." He spoke matter of factly, without expectation, as though this was to be the most innocent of strolls. "I am lucky to have them."

She'd accustomed herself to absorbing undercurrents of censure in most of her conversations. She sensed none from him.

"But families will go their separate ways. Eventually. They marry, they abandon you," she added, almost to validate her own life in some way. "They die."

"I suppose." He sounded thoughtful. "You don't get on well with your husband's sisters?"

She had tried. When she'd received the invitation to stay with them in Brighton this spring, she'd been hopeful for their acceptance.

"I had hoped…" She sighed. "But their welcome came along with the stipulation that I hand over my inheritance."

"Surely, Miranda, you must know Baldwin made a mistake when he left his investment accounts to you." Her late husband's youngest sister, Susan, had waited two days into Miranda's visit before commencing their campaign.

"He always intended it to be put back into the estates," Agnes tacked on.

Because Agnes's son, Peregrine, had inherited the title and all that came with it. Tenant rents provided more than adequate income, and there had been trusts set aside for each of them, but in their opinion, it wasn't enough.

They hated that he'd left her anything, let alone the bulk of his unentailed wealth.

"That *is* unfortunate," Mr. Spencer said in a level voice.

Miranda barked out a laugh. Only, rather than sounding cynical, some of the hurt she felt escaped. She withdrew a fan from her sleeve and waved it below her chin to recover any dignity she'd lost.

Because her chortle had sounded almost like a sob.

Mr. Spencer didn't comment but led her off the trail to a

charming folly draped in ivy and other unrecognizable vines. It seemed to have been all but forgotten by the gardener.

He covered her hand with his, comfortingly.

Miranda was well aware that he had not led her into the darkness so that he could comfort her.

Inside of the shelter, a wooden table split the space in two, flanked by two benches. The vines provided additional privacy, dangling down the sides like nature's drapes.

Eerie shadows sent a shiver rolling through her, and he squeezed her hand yet again.

"I don't know what's wrong with me tonight." Emotion caught her voice.

He pressed a handkerchief into her hand. It was something Baldwin would have done. He'd only been gone for eighteen months and yet it felt like a lifetime.

"He wasn't really all that old. Sixty," she confided. "And he seemed healthy enough."

"His death came as a shock to you," Mr. Spencer observed quietly from beside her. His presence inexplicably wrapped around her like a warm blanket.

"It did." She sniffed. "But he's been gone almost two years. I ought to stop missing him by now, really." Baldwin had been good to her and, in turn, she'd done everything she could to make him happy.

He had been one of the only people in her life to ever show her any affection. With him gone, she'd experienced a sense of abandonment she had not expected.

But enough maudlin conversation. Self-pity wasn't why she'd come here. And she would feel better after.

She would feel needed, precious, significant.

For a while.

Miranda dropped Mr. Spencer's arm and grasped his hand instead, walking them deeper into the secluded shelter until the backs of her thighs pressed against the end of the table.

"But you did not invite me out here to listen to maudlin tales." She slid her hands up the lapels of his jacket and pulled his mouth down to meet hers.

FRICTION

Peter had considered the possibility of kissing her before asking her to accompany him in the garden. In fact, he'd be lying to himself to deny that he'd wondered how her sumptuous body would feel pressed against his.

He no longer had to wonder. He stifled a groan.

The sensation of her breasts against his chest was even better than he'd imagined.

"Not so angelic, after all. Are you, Peter Spencer?" she whispered against his lips at the same time she stroked the wool of his trousers where his already engorged cock pulsed, eager to escape the confines of clothing.

She rubbed her palm over the stretched fabric, up and down his length, and then in a slow circle. She wasn't afraid to apply force, to create friction.

It felt good. So damn good.

He wasn't a virgin. Not at all, in fact. But more recently, he'd dedicated all of his attention to his music. Any physical release he'd enjoyed over the past two years had come at his own hand. Was this why he'd asked her to follow him into a dark garden?

He jerked his hips away from her. Much more and he was going to embarrass himself.

Logically, he knew there was nothing exceptional in this sort of behavior. Lady Starling was not a husband-hunting innocent. But marriage wasn't in his future, near or otherwise, and he needed to be certain she understood that.

"Lady Starling." He grasped her wrist. "I cannot make an honest woman of you."

She laughed. And if anything, his words emboldened her. She pushed his waistcoat aside and fumbled at the buttons of his trousers. "I am quite aware, Mr. Spencer. And I won't attempt to make an honest man of you. I simply want you inside me."

"You don't have to—" He gasped.

Her hand wrapped around his cock, sliding and squeezing, rubbing, exerting the perfect amount of pressure, promising unheard of pleasure.

Did she think she owed him sexual favors for his kindness? His cock, hard and turgid, was prepared to take what she had to give. Instinctively, he thrust his hips forward.

"Tell me now if this isn't what you want," she said.

Peter opened his eyes enough so that he could read her expression. Her lips were parted, shiny from their kiss, and her cheeks flushed a bright pink.

When he didn't answer, she halted her sensual onslaught and tilted her head back to meet his gaze. "Leave now if you don't want me." Organic sexuality threaded her voice. "But if you do, damn you, lift my skirts and fuck me."

Such brazen language on the lips of a lady fanned the flames of his lust.

Her words were not a request; they were a demand.

He studied her eyes, vaguely noticing golden flecks around her pupil, like glimmering stars of light in a dark forest. What drove this woman? He saw desire, yes, but there was something else there. Something he couldn't quite identify.

"Fine then." She dropped her lashes and then jerked her hand back as though burned.

That was the moment he recognized it.

"No." He did not allow her to push him away. Her wanting him had very little to do with carnal pleasure. Her wanting him was fueled by vulnerability, rejection, loneliness.

If this was what she wanted, what she needed, then he would give it to her.

"As you wish." Nudging her backward against the table, he groped at her skirts until the hem was around her waist. "Like this?" He lifted her onto the surface, holding her at the very edge, hooking his arms beneath her knees.

"Yes," she hissed. Her posture, head tipped back, spine arched, conveyed that she didn't want his kiss. She didn't need seduction.

He braced himself, widening his stance and hovering the tip of his cock at her entrance.

"Do it." She pulsed against him. "Now."

Desperation hovered in the air around him; her need was a tangible thing. Power surged through him—the sort of power he normally only ever experienced while performing a difficult run that he'd mastered.

Peter pushed between her silken petals and gloried in the sensation of wet, velvet heat. She stiffened, and he paused so her body could adjust to his girth.

"Don't stop," she all but begged. Her inner muscles throbbed around him.

Her expression oddly reminded of a night he and a few other gents had stumbled into an opium den. They hadn't remained for long, wise enough not to flirt with the milk of the poppy. But in those brief moments, the aura of pain in that room nearly overwhelmed him.

Emptiness. Misery. Hopelessness.

He inched forward, deeper, and a bead of sweat slid down the side of his face. A second bead burned one of his eyes.

Her legs clamped around him, a vice around his waist, drawing him inside in an almost violent surge. "More."

He met hers with a thrust of his own. *Sweet mother of God.*

"Yes."

And then another.

Heaven. Completion.

The sensual warmth surrounding him was a reminder that he'd gone far too long without a woman. He'd allowed only his music to absorb his lust. When he'd awakened in the night, disquieted by sexual urges, he'd poured his energies into playing.

This damn woman shattered his delusional contentment.

Craving more carnality, he kneaded the soft flesh of her thighs, sliding his hands up and then clutching her buttocks. So soft and giving. His fingers dipped into her crease, and he squeezed, working himself rhythmically, wanting to draw this out and savor the encounter but knowing that was going to be impossible.

Which it was.

White lightning shot down his spine, and he moved to withdraw, consciously preventing himself from releasing inside her body. Only her legs tightened around him.

Unable to prevent the inevitable, he surrendered to the unique, almost painful, erotic pleasure seizing him.

∼

It had been fast and impersonal and exactly what Miranda needed. She relaxed her legs and dangled them off the end of the table in a most unladylike pose.

"God damnit," he uttered, his hand bracing himself on the table, leaning over her.

"I'm barren," she murmured lazily. "You need not worry."

She'd sensed his pending retreat and hadn't wanted to lose the sensation of his generous appendage filling her. He was large—larger than any man she'd been with. And contrary to his initial reluctance, he'd needed this encounter nearly as much as she had.

Feeling needed was the most glorious aphrodisiac in the world.

He wiped an arm across his eyes, still inside of her, relaxed, catching his breath.

But he was also regretful. Remorse creased his brow. Any second now, he would slide out and step away, leaving her satisfied but also empty again.

He might offer his apologies. He would locate a handkerchief and after a few cleansing strokes over his deflated cock, tuck it away and offer to escort her back to the ballroom.

She would decline, of course, as she always did, and

sneak around to the front of the manor where she would then locate her driver.

But until he left, she would absorb his weight. His breathing slowed but he didn't move.

"Are you all right?" she asked after at least a minute of silence. Perhaps he'd strained a muscle. Baldwin had hurt his back once... during. It wasn't unheard of.

"I don't even know your given name." His voice rumbled in the quiet.

Miranda opened her eyes, searching for that regret, and then feeling almost uncomfortable when she didn't find it.

"Or would you prefer I continue addressing you as Lady Starling?" The left corner of his mouth tipped up.

Cold filled her veins.

"Miranda," she answered. But it didn't matter.

"A pleasure to make your acquaintance, Miranda."

"Is that what this is called now?" She feigned nonchalance, trapped by his gaze even more so than his body, which for all intents and purposes, pinned her to the table.

Awkwardness settled on the silence that followed.

She inhaled and noticed the aroma of his cologne, clean and leathery, of the grass that surrounded the folly, which must have been cut earlier that day, of a lemon oil that must have been used to polish the table beneath her.

And laced within all of those, the unmistakable scent of sex.

An owl hooted nearby, and the distant murmurs of guests making inane conversation muddled together into a low rumble of meaninglessness.

He shifted slightly, and she prepared herself for a cool rush of air. But she was to be disappointed again.

Gentle fingers traced the edge of her face. "I would like to become better acquainted with you, Miranda."

She dropped her gaze to his lips, which were full and unlined—sensual. He'd tasted clean and fresh when she'd kissed him. The slightest hint of a shadow showed on his chin and jaw, and just above his mouth. He was younger than her. Not by much but enough. And he was sweet.

Too sweet.

"Your sister mentioned you were leaving London in a few days—that you've been selected as one of Sir Bickford-Crowdon's protégés." Ironically enough, in Brighton. She would make it known that she knew he would be leaving. She had no expectations.

He nodded slowly, still watching her. "Being selected is a great honor."

He still hadn't moved off of her. Miranda lifted her stockinged feet to the table, having lost her slippers during their joining, and braced them against the surface.

The effect left her cradling him between her knees.

"I have three days before I leave. Allow me to take you driving tomorrow afternoon." He was younger than her but he was a grown man.

And his scrutiny unnerved her. The oddly formal request to take her driving while intimately joined made her squirm. And yet, there was nothing exceptional in it. And he was leaving London soon. Very soon.

"If you wish." She wasn't averse to appearing in public with a gentleman who was also her lover. Being a part of society often demanded that. But a warning rang in the back of her conscience—*he is Peter Spencer, a Ravensdale.*

And she barely existed on the fringes.

"It's not necessary," she added, shifting her weight and dropping her legs again.

Finally, he rolled off her, but he didn't go far. He was laying on his side, resting his head on his hand.

Still watching me.

"What do *you* want, Miranda?" His question surprised her.

She was going to have to spell it out to him. "I don't require formal attentions. I don't need begrudging promises. I simply like this. I like sex."

He lifted one brow but gave no other indication that she'd shocked him.

"I don't need to be wooed. I'm not husband-hunting," she elaborated. "I crave physical pleasure." This time, it was she who lifted a brow. "If you'd like to better acquaint yourself with my craving in the time you have before you leave, you are welcome to visit me at Starling Place on—"

"No." He shook his head. "I'll reserve a suite at Mivart's." He surprised her. "And we will go there after I take you for a drive."

"It's not as though we need to hide from my husband." Not that she had ever cheated on Baldwin, contrary to the rumors she'd heard. Baldwin had deserved all of her loyalty.

"I'll collect you at five."

Miranda sat up. Before she could smooth her dress, he rose as well and pressed the handkerchief she'd dropped earlier into her hand.

"Very well." She did not look at him when she answered, instead, turning away. She tidied herself but was not about to return to the ball. "No need to escort me inside. A path leads around to the front. I'll send for my driver."

He ignored her, tucking himself away and then fastening his trousers.

"Please, go back inside," she clarified. "Don't concern yourself. Your family will be wondering where you went off to."

"I'm grateful to say that they no longer keep tabs on me." A grin threatened to dance on his lips as he stood patiently waiting for her. "I'll see you to your coach, Miranda. And after you are on your way, I'll retrieve Rosa and retire for the evening myself."

Rosa. She couldn't help but recall how carefully he'd placed it—*her?*—into the luxurious case. Lovingly. Would he see her into her carriage with the same carefulness?

She dismissed such a fanciful thought and went to step away from the table, nearly collapsing when her knees buckled. If not for him reaching out to steady her, she would have landed hard at his feet. That would have been too embarrassing—as though she was overcome by their passion—like some simpering innocent.

"Do you require a moment?" He gentled his voice, and she didn't understand why. Why would he care about the likes of her? This had been about sexual fulfillment— nothing more.

She steadied herself but he didn't release her elbow.

"I'm fine." Her legs trembled from holding them around him. "Do you?" she countered.

He chuckled, not quite beneath his breath. "I'm fine as well." He moved closer and leaned down so that his breath warmed her cheek and jaw. "Better than fine."

And yet he refused to leave her alone her as she'd requested, and he wished to take her driving through the park. She ought to insist upon walking to the front of the manor on her own. She had done it before. It wasn't as though she was one of those Mayfair maidens he'd dismissed earlier.

Like the gentleman that he was, he escorted her from the shelter to the main walkway, almost as though the two of them were innocently strolling through the garden.

Almost as though he respected her.

When they reached the path that circled to the front, burning torches at the entrance came into view.

"Excellent. Herman is already waiting for me." Miranda broke the odd silence that had fallen between them.

"Not the ubiquitous Coachman John?"

"Baldwin hired Herman shortly after we married. He is my driver, my assistant, sometimes my protector..." Miranda shrugged.

Mr. Spencer didn't respond, but she might have felt him nod, as though he approved.

Once they emerged from the canopy provided by the trees, she felt momentarily exposed until Herman opened the door, providing eminent escape. Was her hair in disarray? Her gown wrinkled? Did she appear unnaturally flushed?

Without acknowledging her companion, she ducked her head and stepped up to climb into the carriage.

"Miranda." Mr. Spencer's voice halted her. But she did not look back. Perhaps he'd forget all about his invitation to take her driving. He'd think better of it and send his excuses. Or perhaps he wouldn't bother with even that. He would simply not present himself when five o'clock came.

"Yes?"

"I shall count the minutes until our drive." He was teasing, of course.

But perhaps he would not forget.

Unbalanced by the emotions resulting from his insistence, she nodded and climbed inside, grateful when Herman closed the door behind her. She had not told him that she'd changed her mind. She hadn't told him not to come.

He was taking her for a drive. A simple drive. And then another sexual encounter, this time, in a hotel.

She shivered. He would leave London in a few days' time.

And after that, she'd find someone else.

DRIVING

"Was that Lady Starling I saw you with before supper? You didn't eat. And Hawthorne said you didn't make an appearance in the cardroom. Where did you escape to?" Peter's mother asked before biting daintily into her buttered toast. Although a fashionable countess—and not at all like most society grande dames—she was a mother, *his* mother, nonetheless, and would provide all due smothering accordingly.

"Lady Starling requested an escort to her carriage. I accompanied her around front to await her driver." After one of the most memorable occasions of his life thus far. And it wasn't simply because he'd gone two years without a woman.

It was because of the woman herself. It was oddly ironic in that other ladies teased him with their bodies while offering everything else, and Miranda did quite the opposite.

"Poor dear." His mother's response ought not to have surprised him. Although she was one of the *ton's* most powerful ladies as the Countess of Ravensdale, she'd been born into the lower classes, which gave her an insight into people that others lacked.

"Why would you say that?" Miranda was vulnerable but not powerless. Imagining her lying beside him on that damned uncomfortable table, the odd sense that she was simply a little out of tune niggled at him.

"Lord Pratt, her father, was an emotionless tyrant." She frowned. "My understanding is that he all but sold her to Lord Starling. Lucky for her, Starling was a decent man. I believe he might even have loved her."

"Where is her father now?" She'd admitted that she hadn't any siblings, nor her mother.

"Died shortly after she married. Hand me the tea, will you, dear?"

Before Peter could reach it, one of the footmen stepped forward and poured it into his mother's cup. Peter bit back other questions, curious to know more about Miranda but wanting to learn such things from the lady herself.

"Has Stone already left for Jackson's?" When not in London, his brother spent most of his time overseeing their father's estates, along with the oldest of his brothers, Roman, his father's heir. But whenever Stone was in London, if not carousing with other like gentlemen, he could be found sparring at Gentleman Jackson's Boxing Salon.

"Oh, good lord. You don't know? He's gone in search of Lady Tabetha on behalf of Westerley. It's possible that she's run off with the Duke of Culpepper to Gretna Green. That girl! I've never met one who is more title hungry. All hush-hush, though. Of course."

Peter raised his brows. His brother had been keeping

tabs on the young woman at the request of her brother, Lord Westerley. Likely, there was a good deal more to that story than his mother knew.

"Ah. Well then. I suppose I won't have to endure the night of carousing that he's promised me." Which was just as well. "Drinking and brothels—"

"I've no need to hear such details." His mother made a face and Peter chuckled.

"If you'll excuse me, Mother, Rosa beckons from the music room." Although not as persistently as normal, having been quieted some by sensual recollections of the night before. Even so, he needed to perfect the pieces Sir Bickford-Crowden expected him to know when he arrived.

And besides the ever-present need to practice, it was perhaps best that he spent as little time as possible alone with his mother. She had an uncanny ability to extract information he had no intention of sharing—private information. And he wouldn't put it past her to do that this morning.

"I'm going to miss you, my love. Perhaps your father and I can travel down to Brighton for a few weeks after the Season ends."

A lump formed in his throat at the reminder. He wasn't leaving London to get away from his family. He was leaving because he needed to be better. It was that part of the "more" he sought. He'd not entered the church or the army as many second and third sons did. At the very least, he wanted to prove that his decision to pursue music had been the right one.

"I'm not sure I'll have time to spare, but I imagine even Sir Bickford-Crowden must allow his apprentices time to eat." He grinned.

"Of course, he will. And, Peter?" She stopped him again.

"Yes, Mother?"

"Give Lady Starling my best if you see her again." A gleam sparkled in his mother's eyes. "And tell her I'd love her to come for tea when she has a free afternoon." She lowered her cup back to the saucer. In less than two minutes, his mother had sniffed out his interest in the widow.

This, he reminded himself, was why he would take Miranda to a hotel.

∼

"Mr. Spencer."

Peter turned from the window in the elegantly furnished drawing room, having waited nearly half an hour for Miranda to appear.

"I was beginning to think you were going to stand me up." He all but drank her in with his gaze. The wait had been well worth it. Auburn curls peeked out from beneath a jaunty hat that was more decorative than functional. And today she wore a periwinkle muslin gown, decorated with emerald embroidered stitches that, although tiny, managed to complement her eyes.

Some of the darkness he'd felt from her was absent today. She appeared fresh, lovely, and innocent-looking.

"I considered it." She licked her lips. "I can't think Lady Ravensdale is going to approve."

"Well, you are wrong on that count. Incidentally, she wants to take tea with you sometime in the near future." He didn't need to add after he was gone. "She'll send a missive over to arrange it. My mother likes you, you know."

"She's in the minority then." But he could tell that she believed him, and that knowing such a small thing gave her pleasure. "Should I bring a wrap?"

"Only if you wish to show it off. You'll be plenty warm without one." He found it difficult to grasp the fact that he had been inside this pristine-looking lady not quite twenty-four hours ago. He knew her intimately and yet he didn't know her at all.

"Very well." Her cheeks were flushed from his mention of his mother, and her lace gloves had her almost looking like a debutante.

"You are stunning," he told her because it was true. Because she deserved to know he appreciated the efforts she'd taken.

"Thank you." She lowered her gaze to the floor. "Shall we go then?"

Peter took one of her hands in his. He doubted his presence was the reason for her nervousness. It likely had something to do with his family. Her affair with Chaswick had been public knowledge, but Chase had been a known rake, a rogue. Carrying on like that had practically been expected of him.

Peter... was none of those things.

And as much as he'd like to deny it, his family's influence in London had grown to almost epic proportions. His drive with the infamous Lady Starling in the park would indubitably be mentioned in the *Gazette*. But most Mayfair residents would learn of it first from their neighbors.

If his vehicle was seen parked outside of her townhouse, he'd never hear the end of it. He simply wanted to be alone with her. He wanted to *know her*.

"It's positively fantastic!" She stared up at his curricle

and then sent him a dazzling smile. He'd not seen her smile like that before, and the effect nearly had him stumbling backward. "Do you race it?"

"I used to." He assisted her up before walking around and climbing aboard from the opposite side. Rather than have Michaels, his groom, ride on the back, Peter had instructed him to meet him at Mivart's. That way, he wouldn't need to park it in their mews. Peter trusted Michaels implicitly. Their privacy would be assured.

"You will drive at a snail's pace in your journey down, then?" she teased, even as she gripped the edges of the seat.

"Six years ago," he began, carefully steering off of South Audley and into traffic. "I had just achieved my majority and was racing against my brother, Stone."

Although the race had initially been exhilarating, the memory was not a pleasant one. "Idiots. We were both idiots. He went to pass, and I edged into the center of the road. Unfortunately, neither of us saw the farmer's cart approaching from the opposite direction. I rolled to the right, into a harmless field, Stone veered to the left. If he'd rolled a few feet more, he would have fallen off a small cliff. Luckily for him, he only broke his arm, and I walked away with just a few scratches."

"But it was enough to deter you from doing it again?"

"Along with knowing he could have been killed, seeing my brother unable to perform the simplest of tasks for nearly six months was a most effective deterrent. I realized how much damage an injury like that could do to my playing. Of course, my brothers teased me to no end, but I didn't care. As exciting as a race can be, acting so recklessly isn't worth the risk." But he didn't want to talk about himself. He wanted to know more about her. She was watching the horses and the road in front of them. "Would you like to drive?"

"I don't know how."

"Now is as good a time as any to learn… if you want to."

He sensed her ennui waging with her curiosity. It pleased him when her curiosity won.

"I do."

Peter placed the reins in her hands, still gripping the leather himself. Over the next few minutes, he explained how to stop and how to turn. After they turned onto one of the less-popular roads in the park, he demonstrated a few more techniques and then relinquished control.

"You have the makings of an excellent driver." Better than that, she was laughing. It was a self-conscious sounding laugh, but it was also pleasing. How often had she laughed since her husband's death?

With the fashionable driving route in sight, she relinquished the straps again and he felt, as well as heard, her sigh. This time, it was only two-thirds of an octave, sweet, though, starting at a high 'C.'

"We can drive somewhere else," he suggested.

She hesitated. "You wouldn't mind?"

In answer to her question, he jerked the reins to the left and turned the horses in a full circle, heading them back toward the opposite end of the park. He'd rather talk with her than make nice for the *ton* any day of the week.

～

RATHER THAN MAKE directly for the hotel, as Miranda had half-expected, Mr. Spencer instead turned into a section of the park that she hadn't realized existed. The road was barely wide enough for one vehicle, and it twisted between so many trees that she could almost imagine she was in the country, far away from the bustle of London.

"Tell me about your marriage." He made his request casually, as if he wasn't intent upon peering into wounds she was waiting to scar over.

"What do you mean?"

"Most of what I know of you is hearsay. I'd rather know you from... you." He grimaced.

She blinked at that. Because of course, she knew the rumors. They ranged from lurid tales of depravity to some so horrid as to suggest that she'd murdered Baldwin.

"I cared for my husband very much," she answered truthfully.

"Did you love him?"

"I'm not sure what love feels like. I do know that he made me very happy. He cared about me and, in turn, I did my best to keep him happy as well."

"Love is a bit of a mystery," he answered from beside her, paying particular attention to steer the pair of bays around a sharp corner. "I've yet to experience romantic love myself although my parents and three of my siblings seem to have discovered it. And I doubt they would feign it. I certainly love all of them."

"I loved my father." The words escaped before she could stop them. "Until I realized he did not love me. By the time he died, I believe I must have hated him."

"I'm sorry. I don't think much is required of a man to garner his children's love. If you hated him, Miranda, he must have been a horrid creature."

"He wasn't horrid to me." She shrugged. Hate seemed too powerful to describe how she'd felt about the man who'd sired her. "He was nothing. And I was nothing to him. Nothing until, that was, he had use of me."

Mr. Spencer nodded beside her, as though he already knew that her father had married her off in order to pay a debt. Thank god he had owed the debt to an honorable man.

"If love exists, I imagine I loved Baldwin," she contemplated out loud. "And I do miss him dreadfully. And here I am being maudlin again. I'm not sure what it is about you, Mr. Spencer, but you have a dreadful knack for turning me into a self-pitying chatterbox."

"Peter." He turned his head to meet her gaze. Sitting this close, she recognized immediately that his pupils had dilated. "Call me Peter."

She thought he was going to kiss her but instead, he turned back to the road.

"And I like listening to you. You have a beautiful voice."

She laughed. It was a silly thing to say.

Again, he glanced sideways, this time only for a moment. "You think I'm joking?" He shook his head. "Your voice is melodic but not too high-pitched. Smooth and rich, with a hint of breathiness, a sound that enfolds me like sunshine on a winter's day."

"I thought you were a musician, not a poet." But his words had a similar warmth enfolding her. "Or perhaps you are describing your favorite wine."

He moved the leather straps into his right hand, and then dropped his left atop both of hers. "Why did you walk with me last night?"

His questions weren't easy ones. She clamped her mouth together.

"As I've only a few days to become better acquainted

with you, I have no wish to waste them discussing the weather." The man's persistence wasn't easily thwarted.

"Why do you want to become acquainted with me at all?"

He sat silent, seemingly contemplating her question. It was only fair that she could ask personal questions as well.

"I think I'd like to be your friend."

Her first instinct was to laugh at that. Because most friends didn't do the things they'd done with one another. Nor did they do the things she imagined they would do later this evening. But before her cynical self could mock his answer, her aching heart stopped her.

Because she hadn't any friends. She had acquaintances, social equals, and servants but no one she truly considered a friend.

Her father hadn't allowed her much freedom as a young girl. If he had, she wondered if she would have been nearly as amenable to his wishes. She hadn't been allowed to mingle with other ladies until after she'd become betrothed, and by then most had all but dismissed her. One in particular had outright accused her of seducing Baldwin to gain position and wealth.

She hadn't denied it because she hadn't understood what they'd meant.

Baldwin had been her first true friend, her only friend, her last friend. Perhaps that was why she was the way she was. Disconnected, separated.

"When my father brought me to London for my debut, my friendships were limited to meaningless conversations with other ladies in between dances. A few of the young women were friendly, but in truth, I wasn't one of them." She was talking about herself again, but he seemed not to mind. "After I married, Baldwin allowed me all the freedom I'd ever wanted, but by then…" Everything was different. She'd never belonged to begin with and after her marriage belonged even less. She shrugged. "I kept myself busy at home. I've accepted a few invitations since coming out of mourning but…" People treated her much the same as they had before.

But now it was because of her own behavior. Because gentlemen gossiped worse than ladies and because she'd not cared to pretend to be something other than what she was.

"Ladies pretend to like me. I am a Countess, after all. But their comments are thinly veiled insults. Always with a smile, of course, and always spoken in the most condescending tone of voice. There. Now you've done it. You've got me complaining."

He didn't respond, and so she stared off into the distance.

And then she lifted her chin. "My affairs with gentlemen aren't nearly as complicated, nor are they as hypocritical. Each one is… a straightforward transaction. An equal exchange involving mutual benefits." She needed him to know that although he was acting as though they were courting, she required nothing more.

"So, you don't want my friendship."

"I didn't say that." But had she?

"You said your affairs with gentlemen were transactions. What if I want more than that?"

She inhaled sharply. "You don't." And yet she was squeezing his hand with both of hers. "You are going to Brighton and will focus all of your passion on your music. You are destined for greatness and then you will settle down with someone of whom your family approves."

"Would you be amenable if I was so presumptuous as to tell you I knew what you wanted? Would you like it if I dictated your future to you?"

"I would not like it." But she was right, although she wouldn't argue with him.

"So, you will be my friend?" He was smiling again. "And my lover."

"Tonight. As for more than that—" She lifted one shoulder and then dropped it.

"Let's take this one step at a time, shall we?" And then the horses emerged from the trees into a clearing near the water. "Would you care to walk a little before we drive to Mivart's?"

His mention of the hotel caused her heart to skip a beat, which made no sense at all. She was excited to be with him but her normal emptiness didn't seem to be fueling her actions as much as usual.

"I'd like that." She sat primly, feeling like a fraud when he hopped down and walked around to assist her to the ground.

"I've never been to this part of the park," she admitted as he tucked her hand in the crook of his arm.

"Don't tell anyone, but it's where all the duels are held," he whispered dramatically and then told her about a few of the illegal face-offs he'd witnessed, one where he had acted as second.

"But you have never dueled?' she guessed.

He shook his head. "My brother does enough of that for both of us. And as I've never felt there was a need, as well as for my mother's sake, I have not."

"I envy your relationship with your family." Before he could offer a sympathetic comment, she hurried on to ask,

"Is there anything you *would* enter a duel for? Anything you'd risk your life for?"

He nodded. "To protect the people I love." They paused their walking, and he stared out at the water. "Or to avenge them."

Peter Spencer was a sensitive soul and not inclined to violence, but the thread of determination in his voice sent a chill down Miranda's spine.

"For Rosa?" she wondered.

"I wouldn't kill for her." He slid his eyes in her direction and grinned. "But I would maim."

They both turned and resumed walking along the shoreline, not going far as to keep the horses and his shiny curricle in sight.

"I have only heard you play as part of a group, but I think, before you leave, that I must hear you play a solo piece. How am I to know that you are not pretending to play?" It was her turn to tease him.

And for the remainder of their walk and drive, Miranda found herself flirting, laughing, and getting to know this young man who'd entered her life so very unexpectedly. And their companionship was not only about asking questions and learning one another's histories but simply enjoying the other person's company.

Being.

For the first time in months, she didn't feel completely alone.

TORN

Peter closed the door behind them, glancing around the room he'd acquired, feeling torn.

After the lovely drive and enjoying her company immensely, almost as though he was courting her, it did not feel proper for him to bring her here.

At the same time, he doubted she would have agreed to the drive if he hadn't first agreed to this part of the outing.

"So, this is what a hotel is like." She ventured across the room, touching the top of a dresser, running her fingertips along the back of a chair.

She was not the same as she'd been the night before.

"I've ordered a meal sent up." He swallowed hard at the sight of her standing beside the bed. Seeing the curves he'd not had a chance to fully explore the night before stirred the most basic need inside of him, but he wasn't ready to move in that direction yet.

Because she was gradually sharing the things that he suspected she normally kept closely guarded.

She met his gaze meaningfully and, for the first time that afternoon, she withdrew.

"Tomorrow I will play for you." He wanted her here—her mind, her heart, and yes, her body—all of her. "I'll have my manservant deliver Rosa to this room." Because he didn't want today to be the end of whatever this was between them.

"You are awfully certain of yourself, Peter Spencer." But she had not told him no.

A knock sounded at the door and neither of them spoke until the meal was laid out on the small table and the servant closed the door behind him.

"I hope you are hungry." Peter pulled out one of the chairs for her and breathed a sigh of relief when she uncrossed her arms and lowered herself to sit at the table. "I didn't know what you would like so I told them to bring us some of everything."

And when he removed lids from a few of the plates, he sensed her relaxing again. "This appears to be fowl of some kind, definitely beef, lamb perhaps?"

"You are ridiculous." But she was assisting him now, revealing vegetables and some mixture that might or might not consist of potatoes. "But it smells delicious."

She tasted everything in tiny bites, making faces but also appreciative sounds when the food deserved it. Although she was a few years older than him, there were moments when she seemed much younger. Her father had thrust her directly into marriage from childhood, not allowing her to experience the normal rituals that came with adolescence.

She was delightful, Peter realized, leaning back in his chair having eaten his fill, as he listened to her share a story about her late husband. And yet only one of her strings was in tune. Because just beneath the surface, tension was building inside of her again.

That need he'd felt the night before. He'd given into it; hell, he'd more than given into it. But was giving in the best thing he could do for her?

Was giving in the best thing he could do for *them*?

And if he did not, would she consent to see him again in the few days before he had to leave?

"You are thinking very hard over there." She leaned forward, having folded her napkin and discarded it on the table.

"You know that I want you." He wouldn't play games.

She stiffened, becoming suddenly alert to his mood.

"But I don't want this to be a business transaction between us. I like you. I…" He cleared his throat, suddenly wondering if he was making a mistake. "I'm coming to care for you."

"But you hardly know me. You can't." Her eyes were wide with what he could only describe as panic. "This is temporary. You are leaving."

"Brighton is not the end of the world. You wouldn't even have to stay with your husband's relatives. I could rent a house for you, but I know that you are independent and would likely prefer arranging your own accommodations."

She pushed her chair back. "Unfasten your trousers, sir."

She did not shock him this time. It was the manner in which she could take control of a situation. And watching her, his blood heated, his cock already hard, he didn't have the self-discipline to deny her this—or, by God—to deny himself.

"Do you want me, or do you need me?" He undid his

buttons, all the while locking his gaze with hers as she seemingly searched for an answer.

"Both." Her throat moved.

"Then come here." He slid down his chair and gripped her waist, assisting her in lifting her gown as she straddled him.

A moment later, he was filling her again, but unlike the night before, her face hovered a few inches from his. He captured her mouth and explored the tender flesh inside with his tongue. When she whimpered as she rode him, he tugged her bodice down and buried his face between her breasts.

"Miranda," he breathed. In a single day, she'd invaded his soul. His music had been everything to him. He'd thought it had been enough.

Had he been wrong all along?

Her fingers tugged at his hair, stinging his scalp and stirring the most wicked of urges. He breathed in her very essence. He lifted her, moved with her, and greedily claimed everything she would give to him this night.

But her body wasn't the only prize he wished to claim.

He was beginning to suspect that he might also want to claim her heart.

∼

MIRANDA CREPT out of the room just before the break of dawn, riding home in a hired hackney, filled with conflicting emotions.

Peter was just so... transparent with who he was and what he was feeling. How was a lady supposed to respond to that?

Safely ensconced in her home again, she bathed and dressed and went over a few bills Herman brought to her. After that, she made her usual visit to the nearby foundling hospital in an attempt to reclaim some sort of normalcy.

She experienced only a modicum of success.

Because even as she assisted two of the older girls with their reading assignments, she caught herself dreaming of the night ahead, and then had to push such romantic nonsense from her mind.

He'd asked her the day before if she had loved Baldwin, and she'd told him she didn't know what love was.

And he touched her. Not just sexually but affectionately, which was more heady than she would have guessed.

He'd told her he was coming to care for her.

Why did he care? It couldn't be because he was falling in love with her. She was a fleeting diversion, an enjoyable fling before immersing himself in his playing again.

And he was only a fleeting diversion for her, as well. She couldn't allow herself to fall for his unrelenting charm and talk of love. He was leaving, and attaching any real emotion to him would be painful in the end.

Not the same as when Baldwin died, but it would be a loss. And she wasn't sure she could live through another one.

Returning home, she polished the silver with her housekeeper, went over menus with her cook, and then discussed her wardrobe with Constance, her lady's maid, all the while contemplating the wisdom of spending another night in Peter Spencer's bed.

In his arms.

She even penned an excuse but then failed to order it sent to Burtis House, where he resided with his family.

And then his missive arrived.

MIRANDA,

I'll arrive to collect you at four this afternoon. Round two of your driving lessons, a picnic, and more...
Yours,
Peter
P.S. Not good of you to leave without saying goodbye.
P.P.S. I can't wait to taste all of you again.

HIS VOICE ECHOED in her head as she skimmed over his words. She shivered inside each time she read through it again.

This note didn't read like a business transaction, nor was this a note from a suiter. It was a note from a lover.

She'd had every intention of making an excuse to not go this evening but as the sun moved across the sky, it became too late to cry off.

Her hands clammy and her heart dancing, she donned one of her favorite gowns, sapphire silk, almost too elaborate for a drive, and then she waited anxiously for his arrival.

"He's here," Constance announced from the window. "Is there anything else I can do for you today?" The maid's expression was shuttered, as usual, showing neither approval nor disapproval.

"Thank you. No." Miranda dismissed the woman who'd been with her since she was three and ten. Constance was proficient and performed her duties without question, but for the first time, Miranda wondered why she'd never hired a lady's maid closer to her own age. Someone she could talk with. Someone who had not been chosen by her father. "Please tell him I'll only be a moment."

Left alone, Miranda raised shaking hands to smooth her hair. This was only their second evening in one another's company, not counting their encounter in the garden. There were only two more nights before he would have to leave for Brighton.

Pausing at the top of the staircase, she caught sight of him before he knew she'd appeared. And when his gaze lifted, it was more than appreciative. He stared at her with tenderness and a shared intimacy that weakened her knees.

He took her hand in his even before she stepped off the last step, and then presented her with flowers.

He'd acknowledged the rational aspect of their agreement but then gone on to act like a suiter—and touch her like a lover. He was making it impossible to not be affected by each corresponding emotion.

Pleasure and excitement from the suitor. Desire and satisfaction from the lover. And the knowledge of their affair's transient nature, from knowing he would be leaving London soon.

"Thank you," she murmured, annoyed with herself when her neck, and then her cheeks flushed with heat. "But it isn't necessary."

"I know." He led her outside, ignoring her attempt to reestablish any distance between them. "But I couldn't help myself."

"Foolish man."

"Foolish for allowing you to drive my curricle." He winked. "Daft enough to put my life in your hands."

And within moments, she was again helpless against his

playfulness, the wicked glint in his eyes and his all-encompassing allure.

As promised, he allowed her to drive them across Mayfair and then back again. After their picnic, while driving past Berkeley Square for the second time, she mentioned that she'd never been to Gunter's. He insisted she take several right turns and return to the square so he could remedy such a travesty. She parked the curricle in the shade of a large tree and when a waiter dashed across the lawn, Peter proceeded to order one of every flavor.

"You must make up for lost time," His eyes twinkled.

She shook her head. "On the heels of that picnic, I doubt I'll be able to move after tasting all these ices." Although, after having a spoonful of the chocolate, lavender, pineapple, and saffron, she still managed to finish off most of the glass full of chocolate.

She placed her hands on her abdomen and rested her head against the back of the bench, at a loss as to when she had enjoyed herself more.

Even knowing several notable members of society could observe them, Miranda didn't feel the need to feign disinterest or boredom. In fact, sitting beside Peter Spencer, she didn't even feel the need to try.

"You will play... Rosa for me at the hotel, and I will lie back on that comfortable bed and nap." She stared at him from beneath half-closed eyes.

His responding glance curled her toes. "Putting you completely at my mercy."

It was to be their second night together—would it be their last? He was scheduled to depart for Brighton the morning after next.

She sat up straight and turned to face him. "Take me to the hotel now."

Those perfect blue eyes of his regarded her intently, not bothering to hide his desire, nor his awareness of her need.

With a curt nod, he covered her hand with one of his and waved over the waiter with his other. And as soon as the glasses had been collected, he reclaimed the reins and expertly steered them to the hotel.

MEANDERING

He collected her shortly after noon the following day and, after allowing her to drive, had her park near Piccadilly Square where they spent nearly an hour perusing Hatchard's together. Afterward, he led her down Bond Street, where they took tea in one of the teahouses and then walked again, meandering along as though they had all the time in the world, stopping often to appreciate many of the window displays and occasionally venturing inside.

She sampled an array of perfumes in one of the shops and, although he offered his opinion, he did not attempt to pay for her purchase. She was grateful that he did not. Had he done so, it would have tarnished the afternoon. He seemed to realize that, even going so far as to excuse himself while she paid for the perfume she'd decided upon. The scent differed from what she'd always worn in the past. It was warmer, with an orange citrus base and soft floral notes.

When she emerged onto the pavement, he pushed off the

wall he'd been lounging against and offered his arm. "It's perfect for you," he whispered near her ear.

She glowed at his appreciation. It wasn't often a woman decided to change her scent. "You don't think it's too subtle?"

"Not at all. The aroma expands when it absorbs into your skin. Like you, it's a bouquet of innocent sensuality."

The compliment sent tingles down her spine. Only… "Such a contradiction. It isn't really possible." She'd embraced her carnal needs and surely, that precluded any notion of innocence.

Didn't it?

Peter slid her a sideways glance. "There is something childlike about you." He pinched his mouth together almost as though he hadn't meant to speak his thoughts.

"I'm practically thirty." Miranda disabused him of such a ridiculous notion. "Five, six years older than you?"

"Only three. But it isn't about years." He raised his free hand, pinching his fingers together, as though the explanation eluded him. "When you tasted the ices yesterday, you finished off the chocolate with refreshing gusto, unapologetically. You are the same with your sexuality."

Miranda glanced around in alarm. This wasn't exactly something people discussed while casually strolling down Bond Street and the topic would be considered scandalous —even for her. "I liked the chocolate."

"And you didn't pretend otherwise. Eating can be as sensual as making love. I adore the… innocence in your enthusiasm… for both."

She'd experienced moments where he seemed older than his years. This was one of them.

"Like the enthusiasm you have for your music?" She squeezed his arm. "You still haven't played for me."

"I promise I will tonight." They walked together in silence, and she wondered if he too was reflecting on his imminent departure.

But then he added, "I love playing. I love the feel of the strings, the vibrations as I draw the bow back and forth... The music defines who I am, and I could not live without it. Only..."

Regret tinged his voice, almost as though he felt guilty for the admission he'd almost made.

"Only?" Miranda asked, aware that he'd tensed beneath her hand. "You don't have to answer, if you don't wish to." Did this have something to do with his upcoming apprenticeship?

"At times, it's as though the music owns me, as though it's taken over..." He shook his head dismissively. "It's nothing."

And yet she didn't think it was nothing. Was it possible that his love for playing controlled him in the same way her physical needs had controlled her?

"Like a compulsion. Something out of your control." She blinked, barely aware she had uttered the words until she felt him glancing at her, nodding.

"At what point will it cease to dictate my life?" he mused aloud.

Which had her asking herself the same thing. Was it even possible? "When the compulsion begins to harm the person. At that point, the person must reclaim his or herself."

"Unless he or she endures the pain for too long," he added. "And they are already too weak to resist it."

They were talking about two very different things, and yet the moment was an extremely intimate one.

Had Miranda endured the pain of her exploits too long? Confusing thoughts raced through her mind. When Baldwin died, she'd endured an isolated mourning period as society dictated. After the year was up, she'd felt ravenous, empty, but with a craving she hadn't quite understood.

Without her husband, there was no single person to show her affection in any way—no one to assure her that she mattered. He'd cared for her for over a decade and had become her entire world.

His death left her existing in a giant void.

She'd taken her first lover by accident, when she'd finally accepted an invitation to a house party at the year's end. She'd been shaken afterward, however, when she realized the affair had been nothing more to him than a means to physical fulfillment.

She'd only had to learn that lesson once—the lesson that she could replace the loss of physical connection with a string of anonymous lovers. In accomplishing that, she could rationalize that emotional connections didn't matter. They hadn't mattered before her marriage; why should they matter after?

Even her own father had not considered her feelings, her need for affection, important enough to address. Nor had her governess or any of her father's servants.

Had the pain numbed her ability to absorb anything more?

She swallowed hard, shaken by her thoughts. "Are you having second thoughts about accepting the apprenticeship?" She doubted anyone else would ever ask him this.

"Not at all." His answer came quickly. Perhaps too quickly?

They both fell silent again when a small group of cocksure gentlemen emerged from the building just ahead.

"Gentleman Jackson's." Peter gestured toward the boxing club.

Miranda braced herself when she realized Peter was acquainted with the men. The more fashionable amongst them she knew to be the Marquess of Greystone, the handsome large man with the scar was Viscount Manningham-Tissinton, and the third—a lofty gentleman who'd been conspicuously absent for much of the season—the Duke of Blackheart. All of these gentlemen were well acquainted, she knew, with Baron Chaswick, who was one of her recent lovers. Did they know?

Of course, they knew.

"I see you've decided to make the most of your last days in London, Spencer." Lord Greystone addressed them first. "You won't find anyone as beautiful as Lady Starling down in Brighton."

Miranda didn't miss the question the marquess shot toward Peter, but when she went to take a step backward, he prevented her from doing so.

∼

"INDEED." Peter squeezed her hand just enough so that she couldn't flee.

Perhaps it would have been better if he'd steered them in another direction, but such an evasive tactic simply wasn't his way. "Mantis, Blackheart, may I present you to Lady Starling."

She shot him a reproving glance, obviously aware that one did not present a duke to a countess. He purposefully had not followed protocol. The trouble was, all three of these men were well aware of the not-so-secretive affair Miranda had embarked upon with Chaswick earlier that spring. Peter felt the need to elevate her standing despite it.

To make this formal introduction, he was establishing that she'd moved on. He was insisting she be addressed with the respect any lady deserved.

"My Lady." The Duke of Blackheart bowed over her hand, and upon rising, glanced at Peter and dipped his chin in an approving nod.

"A pleasure, My Lady." Mantis followed suit. When the viscount took a step backward, Peter couldn't help but notice the black and purple bruising around one of his eyes. Which reminded him…

"I thought my brother was out of town?"

"He is." Greys lifted a brow with a glance in Miranda's direction. And Miranda didn't miss the look.

"I'm going to examine the confectioner's offerings." She stared down at her hand, and Peter released her this time. "I'll only be a few minutes."

Peter's gaze trailed after her as she disappeared into the shop.

Greys cocked one brow. "What the devil—?"

"Don't say it," Peter cut him off.

And uncomfortable pause and then…

"This wasn't from your brother." Mantis dabbed tenderly at the skin around his eye.

"Compliments of Lady Felicity," Greys supplied.

"I called on her to ask if Lady Tabetha had confided her

plans to her and before I could open my mouth, she did this," Mantis admitted, more than a little disgruntled.

"What did you do to her?" Peter asked.

"I have no idea." Mantis shook his head. "There is no understanding women."

"It's a beauty, don't you think?" A smile danced on Greys' mouth.

"And it was all for naught, as Lady Tabetha didn't tell anyone about her plans—not even her maid." Blackheart apparently saw no amusement in any of this. "She's leading your brother and hers on a merry chase—with the Duke of Culpepper."

"Not well done of her." Peter only hoped Stone didn't get too caught up in it.

"Indeed," Blackheart agreed.

Peter made a low whistling sound. What was his brother going to do when he caught up with the defiant couple? "Not sure who I feel sorriest for then, my brother or Culpepper." Because Stone was likely to beat the impoverished duke to a pulp. And then he'd have Westerley's sister to deal with. "Although, I was hoping he'd come to his senses…" Peter had seen the way his brother looked at Lady Tabetha. And although Stone insisted she was nothing more than an inconvenient annoyance, that he was only fulfilling his obligation, Peter had seen something else in his brother's attentiveness.

Blackheart nearly cracked a smile from where he stood, arms folded over his chest.

"You do remember," Greys held the handle of his cane with both hands, rocking back and forth on his feet, "that Chase and Lady Starling—"

"That's in the past." Because of course, Peter remembered. How could he not? All three men seemed to be studying him. "What?" Peter asked, not appreciating this sudden scrutiny.

"You're due to join England's most acclaimed cellist in a day and yet you aren't locked up in your mother's conservatory with your precious Rosa," Greys observed.

"Should we be concerned?" Blackheart lifted a brow.

"What the hell is that supposed to mean?" These gents no doubt would have his back in his weakest moments but they could also be giant pains in the ass.

"You have a look," Mantis said.

"A look?" Peter swiped his hair away from his face. "A gentleman can't escort a lady down Bond Street on a sunny afternoon without his friends having cause for concern?"

"Gentlemen can. You can't," Mantis said.

Greys narrowed his eyes. "Especially not when the lady is the former lover of one of his closest friends."

"Not another word." Peter glanced over his shoulder, anxious that Miranda would overhear any of these fools' comments.

"Leave him be," Blackheart said. Peter met the duke's eyes gratefully. "Let us know if you hear of anyone defaming Lady Tabetha."

"Of course."

"And Spencer..." Blackheart narrowed his eyes. "Best of luck to you in Brighton."

Peter watched as the three men disappeared down the street, ambling along as though they owned the very pavement itself. Although a few years younger than them, Peter had always been welcomed into their fold, like an honorary member of sorts. He was going to miss that.

"Is your brother in danger?" Miranda asked.

Peter hadn't even heard her rejoin him. "Something of a tangle, but I've no doubt he and Westerley will sort it out." But Peter didn't want to spend the afternoon discussing his brother's affairs. Not when he had less than a day left with this woman.

"Shall we go to the hotel now?" Not because he couldn't wait to make love to her again. But because he needed to just... hold her.

That sense of loss loomed far weightier than it had before they'd met up with the impertinent Lords. He stared into eyes the color of a forest after the rain. When he was old and gray, apprenticing musicians himself, would he sit in his rocking chair and remember Miranda as the woman who could have been?

"Yes." She was never coy about what she wanted.

Peter stepped onto the street and hailed a hackney.

IT MOVES ME

~~~

Night had long since fallen, and candles flickered in the room, casting shadows on the half-eaten tray of food as well as the two empty bottles of wine.

This room had become a cocoon of sorts. A dream... a sanctuary where neither of them held back anything of themselves—physically or otherwise.

A stinging plagued Miranda's heart as she pressed her lips against the smooth skin of Peter's shoulder, memorizing his taste. A little salty, spicy woods, soap, and something uniquely him. Her gaze settled on the leather case propped in the corner of the room.

"You will play for me now?" She loved being in his arms but they were running out of time, and she desperately wanted him to share this aspect of who he was with her. Perhaps it would help her understand his ultimate passion.

He ran his hand down her bare arm. "I'm not certain the other guests will appreciate music floating up and down the corridor this late."

"You can play a lullaby." She sat up, her hands still roaming his chest, but then forced herself to crawl out of the bed.

When they'd entered the room several hours earlier, he'd been ravenous for her. It didn't make sense. She'd always assumed familiarity would diminish the excitement of making love. And yet, with Peter, the more time they spent together, the more personal details they shared about their lives, both significant and insignificant, their hunger for one another only seemed to grow.

The realization was incredible but also a little terrifying and almost had her contemplating leasing a house in Brighton so that she could be with him. It had her contemplating notions she'd all but given up on.

He did not act like a man who was ready to be rid of her. Quite the opposite, in fact.

Peter climbed out of their bed and lovingly draped a blanket around her shoulders. "Sit here." He guided her to the only comfortable chair in the room.

As he opened the large leather case to reveal the shining instrument, she was reminded of times in the past when she'd watched him play with other musicians; at Westerly Crossings, the Willoughbys' mansion, and then at a come-out hosted by the Duke of Blackheart. She might as well have been admiring a handsome prince. Dressed in elegant evening wear, he had seemed so completely removed from her own existence, as though he'd lived in another world, in another time.

Never in a thousand years would she have imagined seeing him like this, naked, his skin shining in the candlelight. And his hair was ruffled, springing from his head in places where she'd run her fingers through the lovely strands, the longer locks draping along his jaw.

Watching him go through the ritual of preparing to play, she smiled and hugged her knees to her chest. She would memorize this moment.

She couldn't help but notice the tangible excitement that grew in his expression as he plucked at each of the strings and then turned a few nobs. Did his heart race the same as when he moved in and out of her?

When he lowered himself into the same wooden chair where they'd made love the night before, a palpable energy filled the room.

"Do you have any requests?" He tipped his head so a wayward lock of hair moved off his face. Miranda swallowed hard. So beautiful in every way. What could he possibly see in her? And yet the look in his eyes refuted her doubts.

"You choose."

He blinked, his fingers running along the strings. "I've been practicing some incredibly difficult pieces Sir Bickford Crowden sent to me. And they are magnificent, a few of his own compositions." He drew his bow across the thickest string, filling the room with a slow, rich note. "But as far as I'm concerned, nothing rivals Bach's 'First Cello Suite.' It's hardly the most difficult piece a cellist can learn, but..." He shook his head.

"What?"

"It moves me."

"Then that is what I wish to hear." As she met his approving gaze this time, her heart shattered. Dear God, was this what falling in love felt like?

He tucked the head of the instrument onto his shoulder, closed his eyes, then came to life with a vibrancy that reached inside and touched her very soul. As he coaxed the music with his bow and his fingers, he moved his head, adjusting to the sounds. Miranda stared at his parted lips, entranced while he filled the room with… emotions cloaked as music.

Time stood still until he drew the piece to an end with one long note, and he paused, staring at her.

"Don't stop."

"That was the first suite. I don't want to bore you."

"Never." Humbled, her voice caught. No wonder he'd been chosen by one of the world's most applauded musicians.

With a nod, he dove into the second suite and as he played, perspiration beaded on his brow and his chest. His bare feet remained planted on the floor, and his knees kept the instrument in check. Time ceased yet again, and she didn't realize tears were streaming down her face until she tasted salt on her lips.

But it wasn't only the music that kept her enthralled. It was the man, his passion, his exuberance. And it seemed that the longer he played, the more he moved into that other world again. Far from her and every other human.

He played longer this time, performing the entire piece.

Physically, they were together in this room but in every other sense, he might as well have been playing on the moon.

And when he ended on the final note, he was breathing heavily and seemed to require a moment to return to mundane life as everyone else in the world experienced it.

He had labored at this passion for the past half an hour, or however long it had been, and after the room fell silent, she became aware of his breathing, the ticking of a clock on the mantle, and a carriage rumbling along the street outside the window.

But of course, that was how he maintained his strength and physique. He'd told her that some days he practiced more than ten hours.

"You will be Bickford-Crowden's finest student." It was all she could think to say. After tonight, she would gradually be relegated to a fond memory from his past.

"I hope I don't disappoint him." He rose and, just as he'd done that first night they'd been together, lovingly replaced the cello into the case.

She's more than a possession. She's my life... And for now, she owns my heart.

He had not been exaggerating.

"But enough for now." He crossed the room and bent down, lifting her into the air as though she hardly weighed anything. "Tonight my only purpose is to coax music out of you."

When he lowered her to the bed, she didn't hesitate to lift her face for his kiss. If his music had a taste, it was this—velvet and passion. The melody from Bach's cello piece continued playing in her mind.

"I can't bear to leave you. Come with me to Brighton." Heat brushed her jaw where he spoke against her skin.

It was what she wanted to hear. But... "You don't mean it."

"I do." He'd pulled away to look into her eyes. "Marry me."

For an instant, the entire world fell away, and she could almost imagine spending her life in the embrace of this man's love. She wanted to say yes to all of it. Yes to Brighton, yes to marriage, yes to Peter Spencer forever.

"I know I sound crazy, but I don't need months to know how I feel about you. And I don't want to end it when we've only just begun. This is right. This is good." He was on his elbows now, his gaze unwavering, looking determined and eager. "And you'll never have to be alone again. We will be a family. You will have a family. I have an estate in Essex. And although it isn't massive, it's respectable. My father will be happy for me to settle down. Say yes, Miranda."

In her mind's eye, she saw everything that could never be—children with eyes the color of the sky running and playing, the two of them sitting in a drawing-room on a cold winter night, a fire burning in the hearth...

And a distant look of longing in his eyes. Because sitting in the corner, Rosa would taunt her.

Greatness awaited him. He'd spent his life preparing to rise above the feats of normal human beings.

"But you have your apprenticeship. And after that... You are being impulsive, foolish. We barely know one another."

The excitement in his eyes diminished slightly. Because she was right. Of course, she was right. She pressed her advantage. "You don't know me. It would be a mistake, Peter." She gestured toward the bed. She would make this easy for him. "To leap into marriage, just because of this..."

"But I love you." It was possible he'd even surprised himself with his declaration.

"You don't *know me*," she repeated. Although hadn't she just been imagining that she might be falling in love as well? "You can't give up your dreams."

"I wouldn't have to give them up."

"It's impossible. After Brighton, Sir Bickford-Crowden will invite you to tour the Continent with him." Peter moved his mouth as though he might argue with that, and she shot him a disbelieving look. "You know it is likely. I won't take your future away from you."

"Come with me." He was so full of optimism. For the first time since they'd begun this affair, she felt much, much older than him.

It almost sounded possible. But she would become a burden. And after they tired of one another, she'd return to England even more of a fallen woman than she was now.

His proposal had been made impulsively. He hadn't meant it.

"It's too soon." She clutched the sheet to her chest, needing to get out of that hotel room before she gave in to what he wanted. She wanted the fairy tale with him. Of course, she did, but it would be a mistake. Even if he abandoned his music, he'd want children. She'd failed Baldwin in that regard. She couldn't bear to know the depths of that disappointment again.

He sat up on his haunches, his skin glowing almost bronze in the candlelight. "I love you, Miranda. And I think you love me."

"It wouldn't matter." She couldn't meet his eyes. "Your dreams are right before you. I would hate myself forever if I kept you from following them." Because of course, she loved him. How could she not love him?

He stilled, staring across the room with an unseeing gaze. "I'm rushing you."

Miranda trailed her fingers down his chest. She was

going to miss him dreadfully. How did a person go about falling out of love?

"The apprenticeship ends December twentieth." He broke into her thoughts.

He seemed to be working something out in his mind, his eyes thoughtful, his jaw clenched. "I'll meet you here, in this room, on Christmas Eve. If you don't come, then I'll accept that you don't love me. If I'm not here, you'll prove yourself right. But if we both come, then we'll know..."

"We'll know what?" Because he couldn't come... he would be preparing to go on tour.

"That you and I are destined for one another."

She couldn't help but smile at the romance of it. He was so beautiful, so talented, so inherently good and untarnished.

"I won't come." She didn't want him thinking he owed her anything. She didn't want him to feel guilty when, while sitting with his family on Christmas Eve, he realized he'd forgotten all about her.

"I will come." And in his words, she heard something she hadn't expected—certainty. "I'll reserve this room, number eight, for Christmas Eve of this year."

How could she deny him this? Such a foolish promise, though, might make their goodbye less final. To imagine this attachment they'd developed wasn't on the cusp of breaking forever.

Would making such a promise to him cause her more pain in the future?

She wouldn't come.

She would not.

But what if she did? And he didn't? She couldn't bear that.

"Very well," she said.

Peter stuck out his arm and clasped her hand in his. But whereas she thought he was going to shake it, to seal their bargain, he instead pulled her back onto the bed.

Because the future held only a glimmer of hope.

But they still had tonight.

REMEMBER ME

◈

Miranda didn't believe him. Peter could see it in her eyes, in the way she seemed to draw into herself.

He could teach her how to trust, and he would. And he would also teach her to embrace possibilities.

Unlike her father, his parents had raised him to believe he could control the outcome of his life, to believe that if something was important enough, and if he was willing to make the necessary sacrifices, he only required a little luck to ensure the desired outcome would come to pass.

She dropped the blanket from her shoulders, naked and proud—breathtakingly beautiful—and climbed onto the bed. Silken red hair caressed her shoulders, her back. Ruby lips parted softly and a soft flush blossomed in her cheeks. Sitting on what he now considered to be "their" bed, she lifted her arms and beckoned to him.

Not yet. He shook his head. "Let me look at you." If he was an artist, he would paint her like this.

She gave a few slow blinks, but with just the slightest

hesitation, she complied, reclining onto her back, one leg bent at the knee, her gorgeous hair splayed on the pillow behind her.

For as long as he lived, her beauty would go unrivaled.

Peter was optimistic, hopeful that come winter he could convince her to embark on a life with him, but something was holding her back. She was holding herself back. She'd been betrayed, not only by people in her life but by life itself.

To protect herself, she would try to forget him.

He would speak to her in the language she knew best. He give everything he had to make forgetting him impossible.

Rather than lie beside her, he crawled around so that he was kneeling at her feet.

"So pretty—everywhere." He lifted one foot and placed a slow kiss on her delicate arch.

"Peter." A low 'F.' Uncertain.

Aroused.

He kissed every toe, and then around her ankle, massaging the muscles in her calf, occasionally allowing his hands to drift higher on her leg. And then the other foot. Smoothing his hands along her heel. "Precious to me."

She watched him, looking almost pained, until her lids grew heavy. "Peter."

"Yes." He dropped to his elbows, and she widened her knees in an invitation. Eyeing her thighs, he edged forward.

"As I said. So damn pretty." She was pink and swollen and glistening for him. He licked his lips. Already, he sensed her yearning—aching. He would make her tremble.

Leaning forward, he dragged his mouth along her seam and inhaled. She groaned even though his lips barely touched her. "I love you, Miranda." If it took him all night, he was going to make damn sure she didn't doubt his feelings for her.

He trailed one hand low on her belly.

"You love *this*," she said. Even now, she would argue with him.

He chuckled. Because *this* was her. Because he knew her better than she thought he did.

He dropped his mouth to the skin just above her clitoris and agreed. "I love this with *you*." He drew small circles around her navel, and then dragged his tongue down to the swollen nub.

But before he became too absorbed, he dragged his mouth back up again.

"Peter," she protested when he lazily explored the skin that stretched between her thigh and hip.

"I love you everywhere." Rounded hips, a dimple on one thigh.

She squirmed beneath him and he cupped her sex, applying just enough pressure to still her. "Not just here." He pressed against her opening, and his control nearly snapped when her juices covered his palm.

He rubbed harder. Friction. The perfect friction.

"Oh, God, Peter." Her thighs trembled, and she would be bucking if he wasn't holding her down. "Do it. For God's sake, Peter. I want you now."

She'd used it as an escape for too long.

Frustrated in more ways than one, he released his hold and crawled higher on the bed.

Don't forget me.

Holding her gaze, he claimed her mouth with his, resisting his own instinct to lower himself, battling his craving to settle in between her legs.

Exploring her mouth, he became lost in her, feeling her emotions, knowing her thoughts, claiming her heart.

"You love me." He sucked and thrust with his tongue, catching the small cry she uttered.

He wanted inside of her. All of him. Inside of her.

Her lovely legs were wrapped around his waist, tugging, clinging.

She wanted him, he knew, but was terrified of claiming one person forever.

He pinched one of her breasts, flattened his palm against it, and spread her juices over the taut nipple.

"I love all of you, damn it, Miranda." Her ribcage expanded beneath his hand. Her soft cheek tasted like honey. She shivered as he kissed a tender spot behind her ear. She thrust her hips into his hand where he would explore her most intimate sanctuary.

Slick folds—soft lips—guarding her center. His own sex throbbed, aching to claim her. He rubbed his thumb over the sensitive flesh he would taste again later and then claimed her mouth with his again.

Her gasp—staccato bursts, not quite a 'C' sharp.

He slid two fingers inside, and then out again, hovering —denying them both—and ending the kiss on a soft sigh.

The doubt in her eyes made him feel like crying.

She was so much stronger than she realized. Powerful in ways she couldn't see. And despite all the pain she'd known in her life, her heart was whole. It was whole, and it was his.

"I love you," he whispered. "And you love me."

She blinked slowly and then dipped her chin.

Yes.

Something sad lurked in her eyes but also something else.

"Yes?"

"Yes." She dipped her chin again.

The word hovered in the air between them.

"I will be here. I will come," he insisted.

"I know." And then as though tortured, she closed her eyes and tugged his mouth back to hers. This time, Peter lowered his body, sinking both of them into the mattress and sinking inside of her at the same time.

He'd run out of time. Had he tuned some of her strings? It was something but… as a musician, he knew that strings required tuning over and over again.

Her heat surrounded his cock. Her taste filled his mouth. He touched her with his body from the tips of their toes to their lips and cheeks and foreheads.

Deeper. He withdrew and then entered again, going deeper. And then he went deeper still. All the while her legs and arms locked onto him.

This was right.

This was love.

For the first time in his life, he knew exactly what he wanted.

SHIFTING HEARTS

Miranda had convinced herself that her life could go back to normal after Peter Spencer moved on. She could not have been more wrong.

Because she had changed. Before knowing Peter, she hadn't believed there was goodness in the world—not in her world anyway. And even though she deeply mourned the loss of him, something had shifted in her heart. It was as though the world was cast in a subtly different light.

Seeing all of it thusly was encouraging but also slightly terrifying. Because this vague sense of hope he left—hope that her life could be different than she'd imagined—left her open to the possibility of great disappointment.

With her walls beginning to crumble, invitations she received didn't leave her feeling as suspicious as they had before.

Until, that was, exactly ten days after she'd kissed him goodbye, she received an invitation to tea from his mother, Lady Ravensdale.

But the timing was ominous. Did she intend to question Miranda about her association with her angelic son? That would be humiliating, indeed.

Staring at herself in the mirror, contemplating the gowns her maid had laid out for her to select from for the visit, she shivered.

In the past, she would have fortified her resolve, erected invisible barriers around herself before meeting with another lady like this. She would have gone prepared with sarcasm and rebuffs.

But this was Peter's mother. She wanted the woman to… like her.

Not because she needed to impress Lady Ravensdale, but because Miranda *was tired.*

And because in seeing the good in the world, she also sensed that there might be some goodness in the woman who'd raised Peter Spencer.

Miranda was a *worthwhile* person. And she thought she might even be able to be a good friend. Perhaps putting Peter's needs before hers had something to do with it. Perhaps the change came from knowing she wasn't completely broken.

She *could* love.

Otherwise, she never could have set him free.

For this important visit, she settled on a simple mauve muslin with an embroidered bodice and puffed three-quarter sleeves. And of course, she wore the matching hat with silk roses, even though she'd have to remove it once she got there. No lady would deny that an elegant ensemble could do wonders in dispelling a little nervous trepidation.

She lifted her chin as she followed the Ravensdale butler and was ushered into the perfect withdrawing room.

"Welcome, Lady Starling! You are positively stunning in that gown!" Lady Hawthorne, the countess's daughter, gushed before Miranda had barely entered the room.

From the moment she'd stepped inside, the visit proved to be most enjoyable and not at all uncomfortable. She was not Lady Ravensdale's only guest. In addition to Lady Hawthorne, Lady Darlington—the countess's daughter-in-law—sat prettily beside their hostess. Lady Hawthorne immediately demanded Miranda address her as Natalie, and the other woman insisted she be called Rose. The two ladies' appearances contrasted in all ways except for their inviting smiles. Whereas Natalie had golden locks pinned atop her head and an upturned nose, Rose, who, before marrying Lord Darlington had been a lady's maid, wore her sable hair in an elegant chignon.

Initially, they discussed the latest *on dit* but quickly became bored with mundane gossip and moved to discussing gardening and shopping and their favorite recipes.

And when they'd tired of those subjects, Natalie shared the latest exploit of her oldest son. "Brody tried not to cry but I could tell by the look in his eyes that he was frightened. And Garrett and I were besides ourselves!" Apparently, the Sunday before, their six-year-old son had gotten a small toy soldier stuck in his nose. "And my child insisted he hadn't placed it up there himself, but that he'd thrown it into the air and it landed in his nostril." Natalie rolled her eyes while she complained but it was obvious that she doted on all her children. "After hours of poking around up there, Garrett finally got it out by using a pinching device he'd devised with two of my crochet hooks."

"My poor Brody," Lady Ravensdale commiserated for her grandson.

"I doubt he'll do that again." Rose shook her head in sympathy.

Miranda bit her lip. This family loved children.

"You are welcome to laugh. And honestly, he truly expected me to believe the toy just fell into his tiny, barely-there nostril. The imp is lucky we got it out."

"You'll have to warn Benjamin. My poor little Brody," Lady Ravensdale inserted yet again. She obviously doted on all of her grandchildren. "In fact, you need to have Nurse remove any other similarly sized toys from the nursery."

Miranda met Lady Hawthorne's gaze, and they both smiled. The children, it seemed, could do no wrong in the eyes of their grandmother...

Miranda glanced at the clock on the mantle. "I've had a wonderful time, and I refuse to outstay my welcome."

"You could never do that, Miranda," Natalie said.

Miranda smoothed her skirts and as she moved to rise, the countess's next words turned her blood to ice.

"I understand you became acquainted with my middle child, my Peter, before he abandoned us to enrich his musical talents in Brighton."

Miranda inhaled and then nearly stopped breathing altogether while she searched her mind for any of the appropriate responses she'd conceived earlier.

My Peter. The countess obviously doted on her grown children as well.

"He taught me how to drive." The words tumbled past Miranda's lips before she could consider them. "We are friends."

"I'd anticipated that he'd lock himself away with his cello

until the moment he had to leave London, and yet he did not. In fact, he hardly practiced at all that week." Lady Ravensdale wasn't criticizing, but she seemed to be fishing for information.

"I had the music room all to myself," offered Rose, whom Miranda had learned played the pianoforte. "So very unlike him."

"He wasn't all sensitive and broody, either, like he was before the audition," Natalie said.

Miranda swallowed hard. She could hardly confess to spending most of that time alone with him, nor could she tell them half of what they'd been up to.

Or that she missed him even more than she'd expected and craved to hear how he was faring in Brighton.

Miranda forcibly tamped down all the questions she wanted to ask about him. About his childhood, what he'd been like growing up… And although both his sister and his mother were fair-haired, Miranda recognized similarities in their features and some of their gestures.

Lady Ravensdale reached inside of one of her sleeves and withdrew a folded sheet of parchment. "He's written already. I hadn't expected to hear from him so soon."

"What does he say? Is Sir Bickford-Crowden the dragon Peter thought he would be?" Natalie leaned forward.

Peter.

"He says the schedule is rigorous. But assures me he is eating sufficiently." His mother donned a pair of spectacles and settled them onto her nose. "And oddly enough…" She stared over the glasses at Miranda. "He requested that I ensure this was delivered to you."

Miranda wondered if they could actually hear her heart beating as she reached out with a shaking hand to accept the envelope. The younger ladies' eyes had widened in surprise—accompanied by a healthy dose of curiosity.

Miranda would not attempt to read the missive in their presence, despite the thousands of questions behind the three pairs of eyes gazing at her.

"Thank you." Her voice shook as she tucked it into her own sleeve and rose. "And thank you for tea." She knew they were hoping for some sort of explanation and part of her wanted to strangle Peter for putting her in this position.

At the same time, she was dying to read what he'd written. Did he wish to dissolve the bargain he'd made? Had he met someone else?

But the memory of that last night together haunted her.

He loved her. He'd told her over and over again.

And then he'd shown her.

By the time she was home, she could barely contain herself and, after handing off her hat and reticule, locked herself in her favorite drawing room and rushed to the window, throwing open the curtains and flooding the room with the late afternoon sunlight.

She broke the seal, unfolded the paper, and nearly swooned when she caught a whiff of his scent. Leather, spice, wood, and lemon oil.

DEAR MIRANDA,

I failed to obtain directions to your residence but I knew my mother would ensure you received this. Stop glaring, sweetheart. She guessed I had feelings for you the morning after our 'walk' through the garden.

And yes, in case you were wondering, my feelings have not changed. Feelings I never expected or comprehended. You've invaded my heart with your smile and the memory of pleasuring you tortures me at night.

I know you believed my proposal an impulsive one, but I meant it with all my heart. I still mean it. And if at any time you decide you are ready, all you need do is send word. Send word anyway. Tell me what you are doing—what you are thinking—what you had for breakfast and the color of gown you wear each day. I am starved for missing you.

I haven't time to write more now. Sir Bickford is a ruthless taskmaster, and it sounds as though I'm complaining but he has a good deal of knowledge for me to consume.

I will anxiously await any snippet you are willing to share with me.

All my love and affection,
Yes, Love. ALL my love.
Yours most sincerely,
Peter Metcalf Spencer

THE MOST PAINFUL LONGING STRUCK—JUST to see him, to touch him, to talk with him. She could travel down to Brighton, surprise him...

But no. She would be a distraction. He'd admitted that his teacher was a demanding one. He needed to make the most of his time under the man's tutelage.

She glanced across the room to where parchment, a jar of ink, and her favorite pen beckoned. Would it be unwise to write him? Would it undo the most selfless thing she'd ever done?

She crossed the rug and grazed her hand along the wooden surface of the desk. It couldn't hurt to write him once. Assure him she was doing well and not languishing in despair.

She wouldn't admit that she hadn't truly smiled until reading his letter. Because that would pass soon enough.

It had to.

And it would, wouldn't it?

BRIGHTON

On his short journey to Brighton, Peter had experienced a gamut of emotions. Frustration, anger, embarrassment... all of which had some legitimacy and gave him cause to down copious amounts of spirits the night before he was to present himself at Sir Bickford-Crowden's studio. But sure enough, as the days passed, the confidence he'd felt when he'd declared his love never wavered.

Telling her had not been foolish, and his emotions were not fleeting. Whereas she excelled at being honest with him physically, he'd never had any difficulty expressing his thoughts, his emotions.

Having played for her in that hotel room where they'd shared more than he ever could have expected, he had wanted it all. And in that moment, he'd believed it was possible.

She had not been ready though. He'd seen it in her eyes and been disappointed, but that did not mean she never would be.

After composing more than one letter in his mind while practicing mundane scales as demanded by his lofty tutor, Peter had finally committed one of them to paper and mailed it. It had been short, to the point, and honest.

One week later, a cream-colored envelope arrived with his name written in delicate, not quite child-like handwriting.

PETER,

MY DIRECTIONS ARE WRITTEN *at the bottom of this page. Please do not send any more missives to your mother, not if you want me to ever speak to you again. (Not really, but I'll freely admit to wanting to strangle you when she handed it over with a suspicious gleam in her eyes.)*

Should I admit that I miss you? I don't know if telling you that is wise. Nor am I certain that writing you is wise. I'm not sure I will even post this letter.

In answer to your questions in order, firstly, I am sitting in my drawing-room, writing a letter I'm not certain that I should write. And secondly, I am thinking that I have never laughed as much as when you forced me to taste every single flavor of ice that afternoon we stopped at Gunter's. Number three: I had toast and marmalade for breakfast with coffee. Number four: I am wearing a rose-colored gown, with sleeves that boast puffs large enough for me to never have to carry a reticule again.

I am glad you are devoting yourself to your passion. Already, I realize I distracted you from practicing before you left.

Although it's difficult to be sorry for that.

. . .

Yours, affectionately,
   Miranda

HE WROTE her back the next day, and they corresponded back and forth regularly for the first two months of his absence. He'd been more than pleased with the connection, it had been a wonder to come to know more about her without the distraction of the explosive physical desire between the two of them.

And he'd growing quite confident they could share a future together—until her last letter arrived.

We must stop writing to one another. This is undermining your focus, she'd written. If any more letters arrived from him, she wouldn't open them. *Please do not expect further correspondence from me.*

Since processing the contents of her letter, he'd gone from disbelief, to anger, to despair and was now contemplating saddling a horse and riding up to London, not caring that doing so would likely get him kicked out of the apprenticeship.

He drew his bow across Rosa's strings, eliciting a loud discordant note.

Did she think that not writing to her would stop him from thinking about her? Stop him from loving her?

The ironic thought that she was slipping out of tune floated through his mind.

"A gentleman is here to see you, Mr. Spencer." Sir Bickford-Crowden's assistant opened the door and then stepped aside.

"Stone!" The dark-haired man standing in the doorway, slightly taller and stockier, but with the same colored eyes and nearly identical features as his own, was a welcome sight indeed.

Peter set Rosa aside and all but burst across the room to welcome his brother.

"This is what you missed my nuptials for?" Stone slapped him on the back, glancing around the stark room.

"More than a few weeks' notice would have been helpful." Not that Peter didn't feel guilty for not being able to attend, but he hadn't had much choice. "Don't tell me you left your newlywed wife in London."

Stone smiled, a ridiculously lovesick expression Peter couldn't remember ever seeing on his brother's face before. "We're taking a wedding trip. You, little brother, are apparently important enough to have been added to our honeymoon agenda. Tabetha is settling in at the inn this very moment but expects you to join us for dinner later this evening."

"Tabetha Fitzwilliams." Peter shook his head. "I still can't conceive how you pulled that off. What did you do, clobber her over the head and drag her to the nearest anvil priest?"

Stone's eyes danced. "Something like that. I'll tell you everything later. But for now…" Stone planted his feet wide. "I've heard… interesting things about you and Lady Starling."

"From whom?" And what could anyone possibly have to say? He'd taken all the necessary steps to keep their meetings private. Not for his sake but for hers.

"Mother. Greys. Mantis. Blackheart." Stone cleared his throat. "Natalie informed Tabetha that the lovely widow is pining over you. She said it was quite obvious in the time she came to know Lady Starling before the family left for

Raven's Park. Our sister, it seems, has become a dear friend to your paramour."

Although part of what Stone was saying disturbed him, Peter's heart all but leapt. Natalie wouldn't exaggerate or dissemble about something like that. In fact, he'd learned never to dismiss Nat's opinion on such matters.

But if that was the case, why had Miranda insisted they stop writing one another?

"I'm in love with her." Peter rubbed a hand down his face. "I asked her to marry me."

"She is that good, eh?" The corners of Stone's mouth tipped up even as he held out a defensive hand and stepped back.

"Watch yourself." Peter stiffened, clenching his fists. Even knowing that a single punch from Stone would knock him out cold, Peter determined that no one would ever disparage Miranda's reputation again. *Especially one of my brothers.*

Why the hell should she be disrespected for taking lovers when gentlemen did it all the time with no censure whatsoever? Not that Peter could change that, but he'd be damned if he'd allow it in his hearing.

"My apologies." His brother was watching him curiously now. "I wondered, but I have to admit that I did not see that coming."

Damn Stone.

Peter's shoulders slumped. "She's refused me—twice now—I think."

"Refused you? As in marriage?"

"Yes."

"Well, that was awfully quick." Stone rubbed his chin. "At

the risk of drawing more of your wrath, I asked Chaswick about her."

"Chase?" *Miranda's former lover?* "Why in the hell would you do that?"

"He's a good friend." Stone shrugged as though such information provided all the explanation required. "It was notable, he told me, that Lady Starling allowed you to take her driving and shopping. There are even rumors that you took her to *Gunter's*."

"What of it?" Peter did not wish to listen to a recitation of the best memories of his life right now. He'd have plenty of time to do that over the course of his long and lonely future.

"Chase admitted, in confidence, might I add, that… over the course of his… association with Lady Starling, she was not inclined to spend time with him… outside of the boudoir."

Peter knew this. She'd all but demanded the same of him… initially. But he'd forced his way into the other aspects of her life.

"She's not like that. She may have been before. It's because she was…" He couldn't explain it, and talking about her, even to Stone, felt like a betrayal.

"She's changed since you left London." Stone shoved his hands in his pockets and pretended to be examining the room's sparse furnishings. "You are the last gentleman she's been seen with. Rumor has it, she's… reformed. A reformed *rakess*?" He cocked one brow.

"People would do well to pay more heed to their own lives and less attention to things they can't possibly understand."

"I didn't come here to harass you." Stone exhaled. "But

our mother is concerned. When you choose a woman over the music room... Well, I couldn't leave that alone. That just simply isn't like you. And now you admit to having fallen in love with her."

Peter rolled his shoulders, strolled back to his chair, and sat down. Cradling Rosa between his thighs provided some relief for the coiled tension inside him.

Although not as much relief as before.

With one long tension-ridden exhale, he drew the bow across the thickest string, extending out a long note with an abundance of vibrato.

Stone suspected a change in him, and he wasn't wrong.

Because...

Because he had, in fact, changed.

His brother settled onto the well-worn divan at the opposite end of the room. How often had they had conversations just like this, Peter practicing and Stone lounging comfortably, staring up at the ceiling? Their lives were changing. Not only his, but good lord, Stone had a wife now!

Peter stared across the room with an apologetic grimace.

He was coming to realize that music, playing the cello, was not the only thing he wanted from life. He was torn, and yet he wasn't in that Sir Bickford-Crowden was already hinting he'd invite Peter to tour with him. What was that old saying? *Be careful what you wish for?*

His gut clenched.

The thought of spending a year traveling with a man who barked commands at will, placing practice and study above everything, both inanimate and living, held no appeal for him. His mentor was a man adulated most everywhere he went, and he expected similar devotion from all who dwelt in his realm.

And yet, Sir Bickford-Crowden was not a happy person. He rarely smiled and had not laughed even once in Peter's presence.

Peter didn't like the man and had no desire to spend the next few years in his proximity. Even more importantly, he didn't want to *become* that man—an angry, sad, and lonely musician.

Peter loved playing, he loved making music, but that didn't necessitate that he turn his back on other joys life could bring him. It didn't oblige him to abandon love.

His love for Miranda was real.

Miranda.

Miranda—his one true chance at happiness.

"I want to marry her." Nothing else mattered. She'd told him she couldn't provide her husband with a child, but he didn't care that she was barren. He didn't care about her past with Chase or with anyone else. "I want to take her to Essex and make our home together at Millcot Lodge. More than anything, I want to spend my life with her."

Stone turned where he sat, rested his elbows on his knees, and then stared intently across the room at him. "What about your music?"

Peter smiled. "My music is inside of me, and it always will be. There will always be venues in England." He laughed. If nothing else, his mother would make certain of that. And having spent some time away from London now, he didn't mind that at all. "I'm not giving up my music for her. I want to bring her into my world. She is what's been missing from it all along." *Not international venues—not prestigious accolades.*

"Is she worth it?"

"I'm not losing anything by loving her, Stone. Is there anything in this world that could convince you to give up Tabetha?" Peter countered.

The question evoked a determined set of his brother's jaw.

"Nothing." Stone's eyes all but blazed, striking a chord of recognition in Peter. But of course, it was the same look he'd seen while staring at his own reflection.

"I am happy for you." Peter only hoped he could have the same.

His brother's eyes softened. "I never thought..." His voice caught. "Damnit, Peter, If I can convince Tabetha Fitzwilliam to fall in love with me, anything is possible. I support your decision whole heartedly. But you are going to have to be patient."

Peter winced. Because his brother's thoughts confirmed his own—even though he wanted nothing more than to pack up and drive up to London that very day. "But—"

"As far as I know, she isn't going anywhere," Stone said. "But Nat says Lady Starling is particularly concerned about your career. She believes you must follow your life's dream and that it is imperative that you make the most of this," he burst off the settee and gestured around the room, "opportunity."

His life's dream? He'd thought it was. He'd been wrong. But his own words taunted him.

She's more than a possession. She's my life.

Miranda had been curious about Rosa. *"But it, pardon me, she, is replaceable. She's an inanimate object—wood, metal, glue."*

She owns my heart, he'd told her.

His music was a part of him. A part of his soul, of his heart.

But it no longer *owned* his heart.

Miranda did.

"The first night... I told her music was my life," Peter uttered mostly to himself.

"Brilliant way to begin a relationship." Stone, who rarely sat in one place for long, punched the air with his right fist, dancing around restlessly as though fighting a ghost.

"I didn't set out to begin a relation—"

"So, why did you court her then?" Stone stopped long enough to send him a hard stare.

Court her? Damn it, his brother was right. He hated when that happened.

But that was precisely what he'd done. He had courted her. He'd wanted her in his life since the moment he met her.

"Because I just knew. She was the one." As much as the admission sounded like romantic drivel, it was true. "She loves me." He plucked out an arpeggio. "At least she said she did the last time I saw her."

Stone crossed the room to the window. Peter knew precisely what he saw. The old church across the road, a mercantile, and just beyond that, between the two large oaks that towered over the buildings, the sometimes blue, sometimes gray water in the Channel.

Hundreds of miles beyond that, the coast of France.

Stone rubbed the back of his neck. "My gut says finish what you've started here." He glanced over his shoulder. "We'll keep an eye on her in London for you."

Dare Peter hope she would meet him at the hotel when he returned at Christmastime?

Early that last morning, after handing Miranda into her carriage, relinquishing her into the capable hands of her protector and manservant, Peter had gone back into the hotel and reserved room number eight again. Feeling optimistic, he'd paid for two nights: Christmas Eve and Christmas night.

In the event she showed up, he would want to have her all to himself for more than one night before traveling to Raven's Park and presenting her to his parents as his betrothed.

And in the event she did not show, he would have the room to himself where he could drown his sorrows without fear of being interrupted or caught looking forlorn and lovesick by any of his London pals.

The second scenario was unthinkable. He couldn't envision the remainder of his life without her.

IN THE WEEKS that followed Stone and his new wife's departure from Brighton, Peter clung to the memory of Miranda's reluctant declaration of love—a nod—and a single syllable spoken softly. As the air turned colder, his optimism was tested by more than a few occasional bouts of anxiety. And yet all he could do to endure their separation was practice and play—channel all those emotions into his music as he'd done in the past.

He'd always considered himself something of a patient, enduring person. How else could he have spent hours contorting his fingers and wrist so that they obeyed his brain or days on end practicing the same stanza over and over again?

It seemed that where love was concerned, his patience did not come as naturally.

His single-mindedness, however, impressed Sir Bickford-Crowden to no end.

One week before the apprenticeship was scheduled to end, the master musician invited Peter into his office, handed him a cigar, and directed him to sit down.

"I've been pleased with the progress you've made under my tutelage," he said, his eyes squinted beneath his single bushy eyebrow. "And as you are aware, I'm scheduled to play in the world's grandest venues over the coming year. Paris, Rome, Athens, and Vienna. I have chosen you to travel with me. You will accompany me on the tour and perform alongside me when the occasion demands it."

Peter sat up straight, reeling from the realization that he'd achieved one of the greatest honors he could have reached at this point of his career.

And… it was enough—enough to satisfy him as a musician.

It wasn't enough to satisfy him as a man, as a person.

And it was obvious that he wasn't being *asked*; he was being *told*. If he passed this opportunity up, nothing like it would ever come again.

He would be relegated to playing in London occasionally, for his mother's friends at their balls, at the occasional society benefit. But he would have essentially already peaked in his field. He'd have drawn the disapproval of the most lauded man in the international music community.

"I'm afraid I'll have to decline."

WAITING

"Welcome home, Mr. Peter! We didn't expect you'd make the trip. Nasty weather. I wouldn't plan on making it to Raven's Park by Christmas this year, not unless this storm lets up overnight." Mr. Thomas, his parents' butler at Burtis Hall, pushed the door closed behind Peter, silencing the blistering wind and swirling snow.

Nothing short of a blizzard at least ten times this violent would have kept him from making it back to London in time for Christmas Eve, even though the journey had already taken him three times as long as it ought to have.

But he had made it with time to spare and not lost a single appendage to frostbite.

Today was the twenty-third. He would purchase a ring and flowers for her tomorrow morning before checking into the hotel and settling in for what he hoped wouldn't turn out to be the greatest disappointment of his life.

"I do believe there must be three feet of the white stuff outside." He was exaggerating, but the butler merely laughed with a twinkle in his eyes as Peter handed over his scarf, hat, and gloves.

"Four at the very least," Mr. Thomas responded. "Of course, you'll be wanting hot tea after you've changed out of those wet garments. I'll have a fire burning in the drawing-room before you can whistle your favorite carol."

Peter smiled gratefully before turning to climb the stairway to the main part of the house. The manor felt unusually quiet; most of his family and all but a skeletal staff would be spending the holidays in the country, at Raven's Park.

He wasn't worried about telling his parents of his decision to marry Miranda. His father might have a few questions, but where push came to shove, he'd never failed to support his children when they'd made less than conventional choices.

By God, they'd hardly blinked when his oldest brother, Rome, married a woman who'd spent most of her adult life working as a lady's maid, nor when his youngest brother married after barely reaching his majority. And his father had encouraged Natalie to marry Hawthorne, despite discovering that the man's deceased father had been a murderer.

Other gentlemen might happily leave their families to travel to exotic places and see the world, but Peter had realized he was content to be the favorite uncle to his nieces and nephews, a friend to his brothers and sisters and their spouses, and a comfort to his parents.

Life was too short to live far from the people who loved you.

Miranda would gain his entire family when they married.

He stepped into his familiar chamber, which had been dusted in preparation for his return home, but did not remove his jacket right away. Instead, he moved across the room to stare out the window.

Would she be there? For seven months, he'd wondered. He'd wavered between fearing the worst and imagining a future with the woman who, he truly believed, was destined for him.

Peter's gut clenched. Even if Miranda did not meet him at the hotel as he'd hoped, as he wished for with all of his heart, he'd find a way to make her his. If she didn't want him, he was going to need to hear it from her own lips.

She had been correct in that they'd barely had a chance to know one another but not in that he did not, in truth, *know* her. Because he did. In every way that mattered. He knew her heart, her soul, her needs, and her dreams. He knew them, he dared to think, almost better than she did.

Because she'd given him a glimpse into her soul, into her heart.

And then he'd handed over his.

He only hoped she was brave enough to keep it. And that she could trust him enough to give him hers in return.

~

"No one else has checked in. But the room has been prepared, just as you requested, Mr. Spencer." The hotelier handed Peter the familiar key. It was early yet, barely four in the afternoon. She wouldn't have come yet.

And the weather, he was certain, wouldn't be enough to keep her away either. Meeting the love of your life after several months' absence was not the sort of decision a person put off because of a few snowflakes.

"My thanks." Peter removed his hat before climbing the stairs, noticing the oddly familiar paintings in the corridor as well as the scent of lemon oil and wax hovering in the air.

For an instant, recollections replaced anticipation and nervousness.

The door opened easily, and as he stepped inside, memories rose up to taunt him. All the doubts he'd done his best to dismiss assaulted him in that moment, weakening his knees and settling a queasy feeling in his gut.

In the corner, the tray he'd ordered awaited him. Meats, cheese, fruits, pickled vegetables, and bread along with a bottle of champagne sat ready to be consumed in celebration.

He removed his jacket and waited.

And waited.

And waited some more.

YOU DIDN'T COME

Miranda glanced at the clock on the mantel, a lump of regret clogging her throat. She pictured the room in her mind—the quiet corner in the world that, for a very short time, had shown her what heaven must be like.

He would be there by now. She knew he'd arrived in town late the day before. Tabetha Spencer had corresponded with her regularly, as well as his sister, Natalie, and likely, without meaning to, both of them had kept Miranda informed of Peter's circumstances.

But she could not go to the Mivart tonight.

She had nearly changed her mind a thousand times. She would simply tell him… She wouldn't even have to do that. One look at her and he'd know… Contemplating the resulting aftermath, she had just as quickly decided to stay home.

Setting her knitting needles aside, she closed her eyes and pressed her fingertips to her temple.

It was possible he had not gone to the hotel. Or that he'd

gone, and finding the room empty, had been relieved and just as quickly left.

Sir Bickford-Crowden had selected him for the tour.

Not that it was supposed to be public knowledge, but the women in his life were not the sort who would keep such news to themselves.

Miranda lowered her hand to her heart and rubbed her fist over it, as though doing so could relieve the ache there. She would not keep him from pursuing such an incredible opportunity. But was that her decision to make?

If she did not make it for him, then honor would.

Knocking sounded from below, and then voices and shuffling footsteps. Miranda straightened her spine, panicked into arranging the blanket she was knitting very carefully to cover her lap.

"I'll inform her you're here, sir. Please wait downstairs—"

But the footsteps continued to grow louder until the door burst open. How was it possible that the presence of a single person could fill a room with such light? Such energy and life?

"I'm so sorry, My Lady." Herman shot Peter a disgusted glance. "He refused to wait."

"I suppose he's waited long enough." She sighed. "Would you be so kind as to have tea sent up for Mr. Spencer and myself?" She should have had a missive delivered to the hotel.

But that had not been part of their bargain.

"If you are quite certain." Herman met her gaze, and when she nodded, he backed out and closed the door behind him.

Leaving her alone with Peter.

He was as beautiful as ever, but there was something different. Did he appear older? Dark shadows etched beneath his eyes—eyes that burned with...

Determination.

Confidence emanated from him. It was as though his success over the summer had filled him with a greater purpose. Something he'd lacked the last time she'd seen him. She doubted that anything could keep him from achieving his dreams. Seeing it made her proud but also left her feeling bereft.

"Would you care to sit down?" She made a dismal attempt at sounding airy, staying seated as she gestured to a tall, cushioned chair placed across from where she sat on the settee.

Noting his cheeks, ruddy from the cold, Miranda resisted the urge to burst out of her seat and throw herself into his arms.

Peter shook his head, giant snowflakes clinging to his sable hair and the shoulders of his greatcoat. He pinned his gaze on her accusingly. "You didn't come."

The sound of his voice washed over her. How she had missed him!

She pinched her mouth into a thin line to keep from answering. Of course, she had not gone. She would have ruined everything for him if she had.

His brows lowered. "You didn't come."

She ought to have asked Herman to take Peter's coat, scarf, and the hat he held in his hand. But she shouldn't invite his company any longer than necessary even though she craved it. She wanted to bury her face in his chest. And then tilt back her head so he could claim her lips with his.

She had so much she wanted to share with him.

But it was impossible.

Rather than sit where she indicated, he crossed the room and lowered himself beside her. Not quite touching but close enough that she felt both the cold from his coat and the intensity of his emotions.

"I understand you were quite the success in Brighton." She would pretend there was no greater significance to his visit. She would pretend her heart wasn't breaking.

She was allowing him the opportunity to explain that he would be touring throughout the year. She was allowing him a graceful retreat from the brash declaration he'd made to her last spring.

He waved a hand through the air and shrugged. "It was satisfying, but I'm glad it's over."

"But Sir Bickford-Crowden selected you." He ought to be excited. "It is only the beginning."

"How did you know—?" He tilted his head and then understanding dawned. "My mother."

"Lady Tabetha." She dropped her gaze to her hands. "Congratulations. It's a tremendous honor."

He had turned to face her, his knees touching hers. If she could only reach out and take his hand, feel that connection if only for a second...

It would never be enough.

"It is a great honor, indeed." His voice rumbled beside her. "Or it would have been, rather... but I declined."

Miranda blinked away the inconvenient stinging in her eyes. "How exciting it must be—you what?" She jerked her chin up. Did he just say he had... *declined?*

"It wasn't what I wanted." He gave her a sad smile. "After spending half a year doing nothing but practicing, playing, and composing, as well as a string of ridiculous exercises in order to prove myself, I realized it wasn't what I wanted. I love my music. I will always love making music. But it isn't the only thing I want in life." Peter scrubbed a hand down his face, and she couldn't help but hold his gaze. "Never have I met a more miserable person than Sir William Bickford-Crowden. Personally, I want more."

More?

Miranda's mouth fell open, her heart suddenly racing. "What more do you want?" Because she was not imagining that determined look on his face.

He'd come here tonight with purpose.

"I want you." His throat moved, and he lifted his chin. "I want *us*."

Her mouth suddenly dry, Miranda's insides shook. "But—"

"I like playing music for myself, for my mother's friends occasionally." Was he saying what she thought he was saying? "I loved playing for you. I don't need an international audience. I don't require the accolades. Our time together was short, Miranda, but it was long enough for me to know you are the other half of my soul. Long enough for me to know I want the two of us to be together forever."

"So you still love me??" The question flew out of her mouth before she could think twice about asking. "You still want me?"

"I have wanted you since the moment I met you. Back then, I was scared to death to approach you. Perhaps I realized that if I failed, I would be conceding the love of my life."

"*Love of your life?*" she parroted. She inhaled and felt her heart expanding as the meaning of his words washed over her.

"Tell me you still have feelings for me." He reached out and grasped his hands in hers.

"Of course, I do." He was not going to travel with Sir Bickford-Crowden? "You do not want to go on tour? You are not disappointed that you will not be playing for audiences in Paris? In Rome?" It was imperative she understood him correctly.

"Not at all," he answered with conviction. He hadn't so much as hesitated.

"Would you want to have a family?" she asked tentatively.

"Not if it meant I couldn't have you." His gaze was somber. Ah, yes. She had told him she was barren.

Last spring, she had believed she was barren. She nearly choked on a sob.

"I love you, Peter, with all my heart. And I missed you dreadfully. But I didn't want to ruin your future. I didn't… I never want to stand in the way of your dreams."

"The only way you could do that would be if you refused me. I love you more than life itself." He squeezed her hand. "Make all my dreams come true tonight. Say you'll marry me, Miranda."

Sensations of both terror and wonder squeezed her heart but she slowly dragged their clasped hands together.

Onto her lap.

And then onto the small mound she'd been hiding beneath the blanket.

Without so much as blinking, she watched a myriad of emotions flash across his face: confusion, comprehension, amazement, and then his mouth dropped open. "Is it…? Are you…? But you said—"

"I thought I was. And yes, of course, the child is yours."

He drew the blanket off her lap, and then covered her rounded abdomen with both hands, shaking his head. "But. When? How…?" His brows furrowed while he seemed to search for his words. "Why didn't you send for me? I would have come home right away."

"I didn't want to—"

"You little fool!" But he pulled her into his arms, clutching at her frantically, and then cautiously, tenderly. "I love you. Being with you is all that matters." He claimed her mouth with his, and all the tastes and fragrances she'd dreamed of for months filled her senses. Oh, God, it was as though for the first time in her life she was home.

His lips trailed a path along her jaw and down her neck, and his hands explored her belly, breasts, shoulders, and arms as though reassuring himself that she was real.

"I can't believe you didn't tell me. Is this why you didn't come tonight?"

"I thought you wanted to tour." But she nodded. "Your music is your life."

"Was my life. You are my life now… and…" He swallowed hard. "Our child?"

All she could do was nod.

"And you'll marry me?" He was pressing gentle kisses along the edge of her bodice. "Because you love me?"

"I'll marry you." She trailed her hands up to cradle his jaw. "Because I finally understand what love is." Those tears she'd been holding back overflowed. "I missed you so much, and I wanted to tell you, but I knew you would know if I walked into that hotel room and that you'd feel like you had to do the honorable thing but I didn't want to stand in your way."

"Never!" He touched a fingertip to her lips. "I'll get a special license. We'll marry here and then travel to Raven's Park to tell my family." Lifting her across his lap, he settled both of them comfortably with surprising ease. "Strike that. You shouldn't travel in your condition. Especially not in this weather. When did you find out? What did you do? Oh, my poor sweet Miranda. You shouldn't have had to go through this alone." He frowned. "You should have written, you minx."

But he wasn't really angry.

She welcomed his kiss hungrily. "You are here. You are truly here." A tiny part of her had hoped, but she'd dared not allowed herself to really believe this was possible.

"Ahem." Herman entered carrying a tray with a steaming pot of tea and various other offerings. Was that approval she saw in his eyes?

After her manservant left, closing the door behind him, she clumsily climbed off Peter and poured two cups of tea. Excited but also nervous—*was this really happening?*—she rambled on, telling Peter all about the visits she'd had with his mother and his sister and sisters-in-law—before her condition had become apparent, that was.

She told him about how she'd learned to garden, growing her own vegetables, and how she'd learned to knit. She had promised to assist his sister with next year's fundraiser for one of the foundling hospitals and had met his niece and nephew. She also told him the different sensations inside—when the baby moved or kicked. And that he'd had the hiccups a few times already. When she realized he was as starved for her as she was for him, asking all sorts of questions, she found herself cuddled beside him again.

The evening flew by as he in turn told her about the people he'd met, about some of Bickford-Crowden's horrid habits and even the visit from his brother.

And growing serious, he described his estate, Millcot Lodge, in Essex. Would it be safe for her to travel there after the holidays? Or would she prefer to finish out her confinement in London?

She watched as he seemed to be calculating dates. "February?" That look of wonder returned to his perfect blue eyes.

In between talking and sharing, they'd occasionally fall silent and simply stare into one another's eyes. Sentences were interrupted as they took turns kissing, tasting, and touching.

And a few times, Miranda found herself laughing for no other reason than that she was happy.

When the clock on the mantel struck midnight, she could hardly believe so much time had passed. Nor could she believe that her future held so much hope.

Their future together—the three of them.

"Merry Christmas, my love." She buried her face in his neck, more grateful for life than she'd ever thought possible.

"You've given me the greatest gift a man could ever want."

"A baby?"

"You," he said. "And a baby."

He gently nipped at the corner of her mouth, filling her heart with all the hope and joy of the holidays. "On Christmas, and always. I couldn't imagine anything better."

"Well…" She closed her eyes and arched toward him. "There is one thing that could make this night better…"

"Anything."

"Waking up beside you on Christmas morning."

"Done." In one swooping motion, he was on his feet, cradling her in his arms. "You'll make music with me tonight, my love?"

She nodded, feeling almost giddy. "And if you're really lucky." Miranda clutched her arms around his neck. "I might even sing for you," she teased.

"That's all I ever wanted." He met her gaze, his eyes burning with both desire and love. "That's all I'll ever need."

EPILOGUE

SEVEN YEARS LATER

Miranda held her gloved hands just below her chin. Standing in the darkness and watching from the wings, surely, her heart was going to burst.

For walking onto the stage, dressed to the nines and looking far more handsome than any man should ever look, was her husband.

Her magnificently talented, incredibly loving, and devoted husband.

And holding his hand was their flaming haired, blue-eyed, six and one-half year-old daughter Josie—Josephine Amber Spencer. Named in honor of his mother, at Miranda's insistence.

Because when she had married Peter, she'd not only gained a husband but an entire family. And although they occasionally meddled more than Miranda would have liked, they more than made up for it in with their friendship, support, and…

Their unconditional love.

Every last one of them enriched their lives to no end.

"Mama? Josie gonna play with Papa?" A tiny version of her husband tugged at her skirts. "I wanna play too."

Miranda turned and lifted Samuel into her arms. Not quite three, her blue-eyed, dark-haired son enjoyed asserting his independence whenever possible. Too much, sometimes.

"Hush, Sammy," she quieted him.

Glancing back to the stage, she watched as Peter assisted Josie into her seat, where she cradled her small cello between her heavy skirts. Then he took his own seat, where he positioned Maria and lifted his bow.

The enthusiastic crowd fell silent.

Maria had only recently replaced Rosa, who Peter had left behind as a practice instrument at Millcot Lodge, and Miranda couldn't help but smile ruefully at the idea that she'd once felt jealous of his instrument.

What a foolish woman she'd been.

Nerves jumping, she watched as Peter glanced over to their daughter and dipped his chin in encouragement. And then with a distinct nod, the two of them filled the auditorium with the haunting first note of the Bach's suite. Music that never failed to touch her heart.

Tears filled her eyes, and she touched her cheek to the top of Samuel's head, comforting herself with the soft tufts of her baby's hair.

Tonight was a very special concert, featuring the world-wide acclaimed cellist, Peter Spencer.

And as a special guest, his most favored protégé: Miss Josephine Spencer.

Her husband never embarked on a year-long tour where he performed for hundreds of thousands, but since then he had been invited to play in Paris, Rome, and even Moscow as a soloist in his own right. After some discussion, as a family, they'd traveled to each venue so that he could perform.

The journeys had made for wonderful family holidays, but once home, Peter insisted he much preferred England, where he sometimes played in London, a few times in Essex, and Brighton, and near his father's estate, at the grand abbey in Bath.

But mostly he enjoyed managing their estate and raising their family, both of which they did as a team.

The melody built slowly as Peter played softly beside his daughter. Miranda doubted she'd ever seen him more excited for a concert. Nor as nervous.

Wiping away a tear, Miranda shook her head. Josie showed incredible promise, even she realized that. She and Peter had discussed their daughter's talent. They would do everything they could do to encourage her but they also encouraged her to follow her dreams.

And both of them made sure she had other interests in her life.

When the third suite came to an end, Miranda let out a breath she hadn't even realized she'd been holding, and, shifting Samuel to one side, applauded softly.

Samuel joined in the fun, clapping his tiny hands against one another. "My turn now, Mama?" he whispered in her ear.

"Soon enough," she answered. "You're still Mama's baby."

"Not a baby."

"Of course not," she agreed solemnly, meeting Peter's gaze when he glanced to the edge of the stage as he bowed.

Josephine curtsied prettily. She'd practiced that nearly as much as she'd practiced the composition.

A moment later, Peter and Josie were striding toward her, her daughter smiling victoriously, her husband's that of a very proud Papa.

At her side, Peter took Samuel out of her arms, instinctively knowing she would need her hands to give Josie the flowers she'd purchased for this oh, so very special occasion.

Wide blue eyes stared up at her, in awe, but also relief. "I did it, Mama!"

"You did!"

Miranda carefully placed the flowers in her daughter's arms and then squeezed her slender shoulders. "I'm so proud of you."

Not only because Josie had played the piece flawlessly but because she'd had the courage to do so for an audience.

"Mr. Spencer." Mr. Keplar, the theater manager, gestured back toward the stage. "They are asking for an encore."

Peter glanced down at Josie. "What do you say, sweet pea? Shall we play the remaining suites?"

If possible, their daughter's eyes grew even larger. "They want more? Are we ready, Papa?"

"You were born ready, love. Let me just give Sammy here back to Mama." Peter winked at Miranda, as he did just that. "And you and I shall whip up some more magic for these people, shall we?"

Miranda couldn't help but let out a laugh when Josie nearly leapt in excitement. Her daughter moved to return on stage but halted when Peter grasped her shoulder.

"Shall we leave the flowers, here, sweet pea?"

Practically dancing, Josie dropped them at Miranda's feet and then, taking Peter's hand, all but dragged her father back onto the stage.

"I think you have a true musician on your hands," Mr. Kepler commented at the cheering and applause coming from the audience.

"I wanna play," Samuel protested.

"I have more than one of them," Miranda laughed. And what a lucky woman that made her. "I'll never lack for music in my life."

∽

"Mmm... You smell delicious." Peter nuzzled his wife's ear from behind, wrapping his arms around her midsection as he did so. "And you feel even better." Her figure had changed with the birth of each of their children, leaving her breasts heavier, her hips rounder. He loved the familiarity of her belly beneath his hands.

"I like how you feel, too." His most proper wife arched her back and then brought his hand up so that it cradled her breast.

Only two hours before, she'd been smiling and conversing with London's elite, discussing garden parties and concerts and looking quite untouchable.

"Come to bed." At his words, their gazes locked in the looking glass over her vanity.

But neither of them moved.

Her beauty, he believed, would forever have the power to strike him senseless. By God, he loved her even more now than he had the day of their wedding.

"You don't regret it?" she asked with that special little tilt to her head.

"Nothing to regret." He closed his eyes and just... absorbed her. "How could I regret a single thing in my life when I have such an incredibly lovable woman at my side?"

Peter pressed a kiss along the gentle curve of her jaw.

"Mm…"

Occasionally, and when he least expected it, she'd ask the same question. Always with a hint of concern in her eyes but less frequently now then after they'd first married, and less worrisome.

During the first years of their marriage, he'd come to realize the extent of her father's neglect. Lord Pratt had been a rigid man and a mean-spirited person. With him as a father, Miranda had been raised without any affection, without touch, without love.

And yet she was the opposite with their own children. And a better wife and a better woman than any man had a right to.

As her husband, he'd provide her with reassurance whenever she needed it.

And as her husband, he'd ensure she had all the security she needed—all the joy, and that she never doubted his love.

Or the love of their children. Even his family loved her. Of course, they did.

She'd gone living with very little affection to likely more than she'd imagined was possible. Thank heaven Starling had been there for her all those years ago—thank heaven he'd cared for her when no one else had. Peter never felt jealous of the love she'd had for her first husband—the man who'd taught her that love existed.

His mother often said that everything happened for a reason. He was beginning to believe she was right.

This was how they grew together. By sharing, by learning, by being vulnerable with one another.

"You think I'm that loveable, do you? Tell me more," she teased, shifting the mood in a far more pleasant direction. An impish smile danced on her lips.

With a cock of his brow, Peter moved his hands to squeeze the rounded flesh of her buttocks. "I'm inclined to show you instead"

She nodded, her emerald eyes darkening in anticipation, inviting him to do all sorts of wicked things with her. He loved her wicked moods.

In one motion, he spun her around and braced her hands on her dressing table.

"Have I told you today how much I love you?" He bent over her from behind.

"Yes." She met his gaze in the mirror again. "And I love you too, Peter. So very, very much." And then arching her back, she also widened her legs. "But I do believe you mentioned something about showing me how loveable I am?"

"Ah, yes."

And as Peter was a hands-on sort of person, he did precisely that.

***

Thank you so much for reading Peter and Miranda's happily ever after! Now with Peter, Stone, Chase, and Jules all happily married, we need to check in on our other gents. COCKY VISCOUNT is next!

Viscount Manningham-Tissinton (Mantis) isn't looking for a wife—especially not a lady who's recently been jilted by one of his closest friends! But when he stumbles upon Lady Felicity, devastated by her broken engagement, he takes it upon himself to comfort her with a single kiss. And then another—until a storm of passion ignites between them—a storm that threatens to forever alter the course of both their lives.

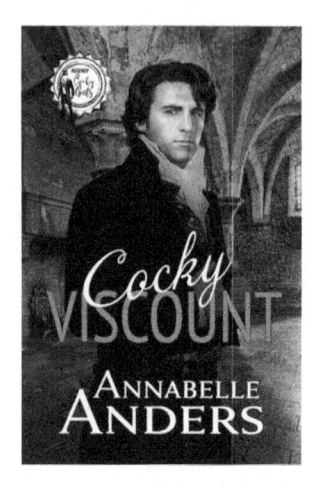

"Loved, loved, loved this story! And not one, but two epilogues!" — *Gabrielle, Goodreads Reviewer*

Grab your copy of **COCKY VISCOUNT** available now!

REGENCY COCKY GENTS

A NEW ANNABELLE ANDERS SERIES

Cocky Earl

Jules and Charley

Cocky Baron

Chase and Bethany

Cocky Mister

Stone and Tabetha

Cocky Brother

Peter Spencer's Story

Cocky Viscount

Mantis and Felicity

Cocky Marquess

July 6, 2021

Greystone's Story

Cocky Butler

September 14, 2021

Blackheart's Story

ABOUT THE AUTHOR

Married to the same man for over 25 years, I am a mother to three children and two Miniature Wiener dogs.

After owning a business and experiencing considerable success, my husband and I got caught in the financial crisis and lost everything in 2008; our business, our home, even our car.

At this point, I put my B.A. in Poly Sci to use and took work as a waitress and bartender (Insert irony). Unwilling to give up on a professional life, I simultaneously went back to college and obtained a degree in EnergyManagement.

And then the energy market dropped off.

And then my dog died.

I can only be grateful for this series of unfortunate events, for, with nothing to lose and completely demoralized, I sat down and began to write the romance novels which had until then, existed only my imagination. After publishing over thirty novels now, with one having been nominated for RWA's Distinguished ™RITA Award in 2019, I am happy to tell you that I have finally found my place in life.

Thank you so much for being a part of my journey!

To find out more about my books, and also to download a free book, get all the info at my website!

www.annabelleanders.com

GET A FREE BOOK

Sign up for the news letter and download a book from Annabelle,

For **FREE!**

Sign up at **www.annabelleanders.com**

Made in the USA
Las Vegas, NV
31 October 2021